HOCKEY NIGHT IN CANADA & OTHER STORIES

HOCKEY NIGHT IN CANADA
& *Other Stories*

Diane Schoemperlen

Introduction by John Metcalf

QUARRY   PRESS

These stories have previously appeared in
Frogs & Other Stories and *Hockey Night in Canada*.

The publisher thanks The Canada Council and
the Ontario Arts Council for financial assistance.

CANADIAN CATALOGUING IN PUBLICATION DATA

Schoemperlen, Diane
Hockey Night in Canada & Other Stories

The stories included were published originally in two separate
collections, Frogs and Other Stories and Hockey Night in Canada.
ISBN 1-55082-003-6

I. Title

PS8587.C4578H64 1991   C813'.54   C91-090147-3
PR9199.3.S34H63 1991

Cover art entitled *The Goalie* by Ken Danby, reproduced
by permission. Design and imaging by ECW Type & Art,
Oakville, Ontario. Printed and bound in Canada by
Hignell Printing Limited, Winnipeg, Manitoba.

Published by *Quarry Press, Inc.*, P.O. Box 1061, Kingston,
Ontario K7L 4Y5 and P.O. Box 348, Clayton, New York 13408

CONTENTS

INTRODUCTION

Forging New Shapes

WHEN I WAS EDITING *Best Canadian Stories* in the 1970s I can remember receiving stories submitted by Diane Schoemperlen who was then living in Canmore, Alberta. I didn't accept any of these stories but the name lodged itself in my mind; it joined my list of the names on which to keep a more than casual eye.

Years later — in 1987 — I accepted from Diane two stories for the first *Macmillan Anthology*, stories entitled "A Simple Story" and "The Man of My Dreams," the latter being the title story of the collection she went on to publish with Macmillan in 1990. Diane reminded me when I was talking to her recently that when I accepted these two stories, I had written her a letter saying that she had finally won through to a recognizable "Diane Schoemperlen story." (I also seem to remember going on to say that she now had to avoid the danger of repeating herself, of becoming the captive of the strategies she had developed.)

When I started writing in the early 1960s I faced exactly the same problems she faced, exactly the same problems that each new generation or grouping faces. The writers I was particularly associated with — Hugh Hood, Ray Smith, Clark Blaise, Alice Munro — were all struggling to create new shapes and forms for their stories. The shapes we had inherited from Hemingway and the other great American writers had hardened into an orthodoxy, a classicism, had become what Kent Thompson

7

called "academy stuff." Those shapes were *their* shapes. What young poet today would dedicate himself to writing, say, the villanelle? We could not write *our* stories in *their* voices.

Each of us tackled the same problem in different ways but we were all well aware of what we were attempting. I would say, looking back now, that we succeeded so well that we created considerable difficulties for the younger writers who would follow us. It would have been difficult to avoid the challenge of stories like "Silver Bugles, Cymbals, Golden Silks," "Walker Brothers Cowboy," "Gentle As Flowers Make the Stones," "A North American Education," "A Small Piece of Blue," and dozens of other immensely powerful and original works.

(I rush to point out, however, that I am not trying to assert the beginnings of a Canadian tradition in the short story. The idea that an hermetic Canadian literary tradition exists or can evolve is one of the nuttier nationalist fantasies. On the other hand, I know from conversations that some of the younger story writers were influenced by Canadian writers of my generation. Just as they were influenced, though, by American and British writers and, in translation, by writers from Italy and Chile. So rather than positing the birth of a Canadian native tradition I'd be more comfortable suggesting that some Canadian writing has moved out into the mainstream of writing in English.)

For the first time since the mid-1970s, I can see now a new formal upheaval taking place in Canada. Younger writers are everywhere forging new shapes which are *their* shapes. This formal upheaval is not, of course, merely some matter of "technique," some sort of nuts-and-bolts messing about which might well provide fascinating shop-talk for writers but which is of no interest to readers. What readers must understand is that the shape of a story *is* the story. There is no such thing as "form" and "content." They are indivisible; they *are* each other. New shapes are new sensibilities.

8

Diane is one among a growing number of serious young fiction writers who are allowing us to see and feel in new way. Other names that spring to mind are Keath Fraser, Linda Svendsen, Dayv James-French, Terry Griggs, Douglas Glover, and Steven Heighton. All are concerned in very different ways with the same task.

The stories in *Hockey Night in Canada & Other Stories* can be read as a record of Diane's struggle towards the kinds of stories in her most recent collection, *The Man of My Dreams*. This is not to be patronizing. The remarkable thing about *Hockey Night in Canada & Other Stories* is that all the stories hold up well. All contain surprises, felicities, pleasures.

In 1976, Diane attended a six-week summer writing workshop in Banff. For one of those weeks she was taught by Alice Munro. Some of the stories in this collection — I'm thinking of "The Long Way Home," "Hockey Night in Canada," "Clues," and "Crimes of Passion" — suggest to me the influence of the Alice Munro of such stories as "Walker Brothers Cowboy" and "Images."

Then there are the transitional stories which are attempting to break away from the influences, such stories as "First Things First," "Frogs," and "Notes for a Travelogue."

And then there are achieved new forms in such stories as "Life Sentences," "This Town," and "True or False."

But even in her earlier and more conventional stories Diane's work could not be confused with Alice Munro's. And as she develops could not be confused with that of any other young writer in Canada.

Diane's territory is not rural or small town but is rather the gritty urban world of the Safeway, the laundromat, the café whose orange vinyl seats are patched with black electrical tape, a world where men dream of women who are "queens" but settle instead for women they think of as "utility grade," a world where women yearn for true love but end up trading gross recipes for Lazy Day Lasagna and Inside-Out Ravioli.

Life in this world bruises Diane Schoemperlen's heroines in their affairs and relationships and failing marriages and they learn and record small wisdoms with a tough, rueful humor:

Last August I met this guy Dean at a party. I remember thinking he looked a little tired but I didn't see that as a serious problem at the time. He fell asleep at the party but then we'd all had quite a bit to drink and he wasn't the only one. He looked like a child when he was asleep. It wasn't until later that I discovered this is true of many people and is not an accurate measure of one's character.

Indeed, it is Diane's humor which is, for me, the central pleasure of her work. Nearly all the stories are marked with a sly humor which is wry and dry and sometimes as painful as ingested ground glass:

She thought of her cousin Denise back in Hastings whom she had always been told had married late in life. For years, the whole family had treated Denise with a hopeful sympathy, as though there were little else she could be expected to do at such an advanced age besides marry a widower or keep working forever at the Bank of Montreal. Ruth had recently figured out that Denise actually got married at twenty-eight. Her husband, Howard Machuk, was a gynecologist who'd never been married and he gave her everything she could possibly want, including a dishwasher for her thirty-first birthday.

Diane creates this world with loving detail and detail itself — trade names, brand names, the banal language of advertising, the plenitude of deliberately flat fact — forms one of her comic devices.

I'm beginning to suspect that she is building, story by story, the Schoemperlen world. I mean by this that as she continues to write we'll begin to pay her the ultimate compliment of recognizing certain things we see as essentially details from a Schoemperlen story. I will never again see an orange vinyl seat patched with black electrical tape without being immediately reminded of her observing eye. And can there *really* be a dish called Inside-Out Ravioli? But one *knows* it's true.

If someone were to ask for an example of the sadly funny world of Diane Schoemperlen, I'd give them to read the following paragraph from "Notes for a Travelogue." Sharon and Grant are two years into a failing marriage and take a week's holiday camping in an effort to hold matters together. On the first night they pitch their tent in the dark in a campground. The paragraph describes the next morning:

> Morning reveals a white Winnebago squatting just down the way, fat with sleeping strangers. There seems to be ten or twelve of them, with interchangeable heads, emerging one by one in various states of half-dress. The children race down to the lake in a pack while the adults put the coffee on. They holler blindly back and forth at each other through the tree cover — warnings, discoveries, the breakfast menu. While I'm waiting my turn in the fibreglass outhouse, a white poodle licks amiably at my ankles. Grant pumps up the Coleman stove and breaks eggs seriously into a metal bowl.

This paragraph is crammed with pleasures: the Winnebago "fat with sleeping strangers," the choice of the words "amiably" and "seriously." But the real joy of the paragraph in its context in the story is the way it seems to suggest and stand for and comment on the state of Sharon's marriage.

Welcome to the world of Diane Schoemperlen.

John Metcalf

Ottawa, February 1991

HOCKEY NIGHT IN CANADA

WE SETTLED OURSELVES in our usual places, my father and I, while the singer made his way out onto the ice and the organist cranked up for "O Canada" and "The Star Spangled Banner." Saturday night and we were ready for anything, my father half-sitting, half-lying on the chesterfield with his first dark rum and Pepsi, and I in the swivel chair beside the picture window with a box of barbecue chips and a glass of 7Up.

My mother was ripping apart with relish a red and white polka dot dress she hadn't worn for years. There were matching red shoes, purse and a hat once too, but they'd already been packed or given away. Trying to interest someone in her project and her practicality, she said, "Why, this fabric is just as good as new," pulling first one sleeve, then the other, away from the body of the dress.

But the game was starting and we were already intent on the screen and each other.

"They don't stand a chance tonight," I said, shaking my head sadly but with confidence as the players skated out.

My father grinned calmly and took a drink of rum.

"Not a chance," I prodded.

"We'll see, we'll just see about that." Even when they played poorly for weeks on end, my father remained cheerfully loyal to the Chicago Black Hawks, for no particular reason I could see, except that he always had been. He must have suffered secret doubts about the team now and then — anyone would — but he never let on. I, having no similar special allegiance

13

and wanting to keep the evening interesting, always hoped for the other team.

We were not violent fans, either one of us. We never hollered, leaped out of our chairs, or pounded ourselves in alternating fits of frustration and ecstasy. We did not jump up and down yelling, "Kill him, kill him!" Instead, we were teasing fans, pretend fans almost, feigning hostility and heartbreak, smirking and groaning gruesomely by turns, exaggerating our reactions mainly for the benefit of the other and sometimes just to get a rise out of my mother, who was by this time humming with pins in her mouth, smoothing pattern pieces onto the remains of the dress, and snipping merrily away with the pinking shears, while scraps of cloth and tissue paper drifted to the floor all around her.

The dress, I discovered, was to be reincarnated as a blouse for me, a blouse which, by the time it was finished (perfectly, seams all basted and bound, hem hand-done), I would probably hate. Between periods, she took me into the bathroom for a fitting session in front of the full-length mirror. I did not breathe, complain or look as she pinned the blouse together around me, a piece at a time, one sleeve, the other, half the front, the other half, back, collar, the cold silver pins scratching my bare skin just lightly.

By the time we got to the three-star selection after the game, my mother was off to the back bedroom with the blouse, whirring away on the Singer.

When her friend Rita was there, my mother at least played at watching the game. Whenever the crowd roared, my father groaned and Rita began to shriek, my mother would look up from her stamp collection, which she was endlessly sorting and sticking and spreading all over the card table, and smile encouragement at the TV.

"Who scored?" she asked innocently, as she put another page in her album and arranged another row of stamps across it.

Russia was her favorite country for collecting, the best, because their stamps were bigger and grander than any, especially ours, which looked stingy and common by comparison. The Russians had hockey players, cosmonauts, fruits and vegetables, wild animals, trucks and ballerinas, in red, blue, green, yellow, even shiny silver and gold. We had mainly the Queen in pastels. My mother's everyday fear and loathing of Communists did not enter into the matter.

"Just guess, Violet, just you guess who scored!" Rita crowed.

"Don't ask," my father muttered.

"Most goals, one team, one game," Rita recited. "Twenty-one, Montreal Canadiens, March 3, 1920, at Montreal, defeated the Quebec Bulldogs 18 to 3."

"Ancient history," said my father. "Besides, who ever heard of the Quebec Bulldogs anyway? You're making it all up, Rita. Tell me another one."

"Fewest points, one season," Rita chanted. "Thirty-one, Chicago Black Hawks, 1953/54, won 12, lost 36, tied 4."

"Not quite what I had in mind." My father rolled his big eyes and went into the kitchen to fix more drinks, one for himself and one for Rita, who took her rum with orange juice, no ice. I said nothing, not being sure yet whether I wanted to stick up for my father or fall in love with the Canadiens too.

Rita had followed the Montreal team for years. Unlike my father and me, she was a *real* fan, a serious fan who shrieked and howled and paced around the living room, calling the players by their first names, begging them to score, willing them to win with clenched fists and teeth. She did not consider her everyday dislike of those Frenchmen (as in, "I've got no use for those Frenchmen, no use at all") to be contradictory. Hockey, like stamp collecting, it seemed, was a world apart, immune to the regular prejudices of race, province and country — although she did sometimes berate my father for siding with a Yankee team.

When the Black Hawks lost another one, Rita and I (for I'd been won over after all by her braying) took all the credit for knowing the better team right off the bat, and heaped all the blame upon my father who was now in disgrace along with his team — a position he took rather well. When they did win, as far as he was concerned, it was all or mainly because he'd never given up on them.

After the game my father and I usually played a few hands of poker, a penny a game, with the cards spread out on the chesterfield between us. My mother and Rita were in the kitchen having coffee and maybe a cream puff. The hum of their voices came to me just vaguely, like perfume. I wanted to hear what they were saying but my father was analyzing the last power play and dealing me another hand. I won more often than not, piling up my pennies. For years after this I would think of myself as lucky at cards. In certain difficult situations which showed a disturbing tendency to repeat themselves, I would often be reminded of Rita's teasing warning: "Lucky at cards, unlucky at love."

Later, after Rita had gone home, I would find the ashtray full of lipstick-tipped butts which I pored over, looking for clues.

My mother had met Rita that summer at Eaton's where Rita was working at the Cosmetics counter. Rita still worked at Eaton's, but she was in Ladies Dresses now, having passed briefly through Lingerie and Swimwear in between.

To hear Rita tell it, you'd think their whole friendship was rooted in my mother's hair.

"I just couldn't help myself," Rita said, telling me the story. "There I was trying to convince this fat lady that all she really needed was a bottle of Cover Girl and some Midnight Blue mascara and up walked your mother with her hair."

Patting her hair fondly, my mother said, "I couldn't figure

out what she was staring at."

I already knew that before Rita had come to live in Hastings, she was a hairdresser in Toronto. She'd been to hairdressing school for two years and still took the occasional special course in cold waves or coloring. She was about to open her own beauty parlor just when her husband Geoffrey killed himself and everything was changed. It was not long after that that Rita gave up hairdressing and moved to Hastings to stay with her younger sister, Jeanette. Six months after that Jeanette married a doctor and moved back to Toronto. But Rita stayed on in Hastings anyway, bought herself a second-hand car and rented an apartment downtown in the Barclay Block above an Italian bakery (which was the very same building my parents had lived in when they were first married, a fact that I found significant and somehow too good to be true).

My mother always did her own hair, putting it up in pincurls every Sunday night so that it lay in lustrous black waves all around her face and rolled thickly down past her shoulders in the back. But what Rita meant was the streak, a pure white streak in front from the time she'd had ringworm when she was small. Even I had to admit it looked splendid and daring, although there were times when we were fighting and I wanted to hurt her and tell her she looked like a skunk. Rita's own hair was straggly and thin, half-dead from too many washings, a strange salmon color, growing out blonde, from too many experiments. Her bangs hung down almost to her eyebrows. Sometimes she wore them swept back with colored barrettes, revealing the delicate blue veins in her temples.

"Anyway," Rita said, pausing to light another cigarette with her Zippo, "I finally got rid of the fat lady and your mother and I got talking. Just seeing her hair gave me the itch again — I could just picture all the things I could do with that hair. We went up to the cafeteria for coffee — "

"And we've been friends ever since," my mother said in a

17

pleased and final-sounding voice, the way you might say, And they all lived happily ever after.

My mother had never really had a friend of her own before. Oh, there was a neighbor lady, Mrs. Kent three doors down, who would come over once in a while to borrow things that she never returned — the angel food cake pan, the egg beater, the four-sided cheese grater. And so my mother would go over to Mrs. Kent's house occasionally too, to get the things back. But it was never what you would call a friendship, so much as a case of proximity and Mrs. Kent's kitchen being sadly ill-equipped.

I had never seriously thought of my mother as wanting or needing a friend anyway. Friends, particularly best friends, I gathered, were something you grew out of soon after you got married and had children. After that, the husband and the children became your best friends, or were supposed to.

But then she met Rita and it was as though Rita were someone she had been just waiting for, saving herself up for all those years. They told each other old stories and secrets, made plans, remembered times before when they might have met, had just missed each other, almost met, but didn't. Rita was at least ten years younger than my mother. I suppose I thought of her as doing my mother a favor by being her friend. In the way of young girls, I just naturally imagined my mother to be the needy one of the two.

When Rita was in Cosmetics, she would bring my mother make-up samples that the salesmen had left: mascara, blusher, eyebrow pencils, and sometimes half-empty perfume testers for me. And her pale face was perfect. Once she moved to Ladies Dresses, she hardly ever wore slacks anymore, except when the weather turned cold. She was always trying out bold new accessories, big belts, colored stockings, high-heeled boots. I could only imagine what she'd bought while she worked in Lingerie — the most elegant underwear, I supposed, and colored girdles (I didn't know if there were such things for sure, but if there were, Rita would have several), and marvellous gauzy nightgowns.

On her day off during the week Rita was usually there in the kitchen when I came home from school for lunch. While my mother fixed me a can of soup and a grilled cheese sandwich, Rita sipped black coffee and nibbled on fresh fruit and cottage cheese. This was the first I knew of dieting as a permanent condition, for although Rita was quite slim and long-legged, she was always watching her weight. My mother, who was much rounder than Rita anyway, had taken up dieting too, like a new hobby which required supplies of lettuce, pink grapefruit and detailed diet books listing menus, recipes and calories. She'd begun to compliment me on my extreme thinness, when not so many years before she'd made me wear two crinolines to school so the teachers wouldn't think she didn't feed me. How was it that, without changing size or shape, I had graduated from grotesque to slender?

"How's school going this week?" Rita would ask, offering me a tiny cube of pineapple, which I hated.

She listened patiently, nodding and frowning mildly, while I told her about Miss Morton, the gym teacher who hated me because I was no good at basketball; and about my best friend Mary Yurick who was madly in love with Lorne Puhalski, captain of the hockey team and unattainable; and about everybody's enemy, Bonnie Ettinger, who'd beat up Della White on Monday in the alley behind the school.

It was easy to get carried away with such confidences in the hope that Rita would reciprocate, and I almost told her that I was in love with Lorne Puhalski too, and that Bonnie Ettinger was going around saying she'd knock my block off if she ever got the chance. But I talked myself out of it at the last minute. I wanted so much to have Rita all to myself but somehow it never was arranged.

With Rita there, my mother could listen to my problems without worrying too much or wanting to do something about them. She and I probably learned more about each other from those kitchen conversations with Rita than we ever would have any other way.

Sometimes it was as though they'd forgotten all about me. One day when I came home for lunch my mother was sitting wrapped in a sheet on the high stool in the middle of the kitchen while Rita gave her a cold wave, something she'd been threatening to do for weeks. I made my own sandwich.

My mother was saying, "I was so young then, and everybody said I was pretty. We were in love but when they found out, they shipped him off to agricultural school in Winnipeg. I still think Sonny was my own true love."

"What about Ted?" Rita asked, wrapping pieces of hair in what looked like cigarette rolling papers and then winding them nimbly onto pink plastic rods.

"Oh, Ted."

Ted was my father of course, but it was strange to hear my mother call him by his name when usually she called him "Dad" or "your Dad."

"Yes, well, Ted. That was different. I was older. I'm even older now. I didn't tell Ted about Sonny until long after we were married."

I went back to school that afternoon with a picture of my mother as another person altogether, someone I had never met and never would now. This woman, mysterious, incomplete and broken-hearted, pestered me all day long. The stink of the cold wave chemicals lingered too, bitter but promising.

At other times it was as though my mother could tell me things through Rita that she could never have expressed if we were alone.

One Saturday night after the hockey game I left my father dozing on the chesterfield and went into the kitchen.

Rita was saying, "When Geoffrey hung himself, his whole family blamed me. They said I'd driven him to it. They kept bringing up the baby who died and then Geoffrey too, as if I'd murdered them both with my bare hands. I had a nervous breakdown and they said it served me right. It was then that I realized I would have to leave town." She spoke calmly, looking down at her lap, not moving, and a sense of young tragic death wound around her like scented bandages, permanent and disfiguring, the way Japanese women used to bind their feet to keep them dainty. She was doomed somehow, I could see that now, even though I'd never noticed it before.

"You have to be strong, we all have to be strong," my mother said without looking at me. "We're the women, we have to be stronger than they think we are."

I could hear my father snoring lightly in the other room, no longer harmless. The kitchen was snug with yellow light. The window was patterned with frost like feathers or ferns and it was just starting to snow. My mother pulled the blind down so no one could see in. We could have been anywhere, just the three of us, bending in together around the kitchen table, knowing things, these sad things, that no one else knew yet.

That night Rita slept over. An odd thing for grown-ups to do, I thought, but I liked it.

After I'd gone to bed, it reminded me of Christmas: something special waiting all night long in the living room: the tree, the unopened presents, Rita in my mother's new nightie wrapped up in an old car blanket on the chesterfield.

Around the middle of December, Rita flew to Toronto to have Christmas with her sister Jeanette and her doctor husband. My mother had somehow not considered exchanging presents with Rita and was horrified when she appeared the morning she left with three gaily-wrapped boxes, one for each of us. Even more surprising was my father, who handed Rita a little package tied up with curly red ribbons. She opened it on the spot, still standing in the doorway, and produced a silver charm of the Montreal Canadiens' crest.

On Christmas morning we opened her presents first. She'd given my mother a white silk scarf hand-painted with an ocean scene in vivid blues and greens. My father held up a red Chicago Black Hawks jersey with the Indian head on the front and the number 21 on the back. I got a leather-covered date book for the new year in which I immediately noted the birthdays of everyone I could think of. Rita's presents were the best ones that year.

After dinner, we called all our relatives in Manitoba and then my mother took some pictures of the tree, of my father in his new hockey sweater and of me eating my dessert behind the chicken carcass. My friend Mary called and we told each other everything we got. I thought Rita might call later but she didn't.

Between Christmas and New Year's my mother went out and bought a braided gold necklace to give to Rita when she got back. The silver charm was never discussed in front of me.

Not long after Rita returned from her holidays, she was moved from Ladies Dresses into Ladies Coats. Now when she came over she wore a knee-length black coat trimmed with grey Persian lamb at the collar and cuffs. She always hesitated before taking it off, caressing the curly lapels, picking invisible lint off the back, giving my mother and I just enough time to notice and admire it again. She knew a lot about mink and ermine now, how the little things were bred and raised on special farms, how vicious they were, how many tiny pelts it took to make just one coat. She lusted uncontrollably, as she put it, after one particular mink coat in her department but had resigned herself to never being able to afford it and seemed both relieved and disappointed the day it was bought by some doctor's wife.

"Just between you and I," my mother said right after Rita

phoned to say she'd sold the fabulous coat, "I think mink is a waste of money. It's only for snobs. I wouldn't wear one if you gave it to me." Ten years later, my father bought her a mink jacket trimmed with ermine and she said, hugging him, "Oh, Ted, I've always wanted one."

It was an extravagant winter, with new records set for both snow and all-time low temperatures. My father seemed to be always outside shovelling snow in the dark, piling up huge icy banks all around the house. He would come in from the cold red-cheeked and handsome, trying to put his icy hands around my neck. Rita came over less and less often. She said it was because her car wouldn't start half the time, even when she kept it plugged in.

On warmer days when Rita wasn't working, my mother often took the bus downtown to her apartment. When I came home from school at three-thirty, the house would be luxuriously empty. I curled up on the chesterfield with the record player on and wrote in the date book Rita had given me or worked on the optimistic list my friend Mary and I had started: "One Thousand Things We Like." Well into its second spiral notebook, the list had passed seven hundred and was coming up quickly on eight with

> cuckoo clocks
> Canada
> lace
> my mother's hair
> comfortable underwear and
> having a bath without interruptions

being the most recent additions.

My mother returned just in time to start supper before my father got home from work. She was distracted then in a pleasant sort of way, all jazzed up and jingling from too much coffee or something, gabbing away gaily as she peeled the potatoes. Rita had given her some old clothes which could be made over into any number of new outfits for me. There was a reversible plaid skirt I'd always admired and wanted to wear right away but my mother said it was too old for me.

One Saturday afternoon when we had been out shopping together, my mother suggested we drop in on Rita before catching the bus home. I had never been to her apartment before and as we walked up Northern Avenue to the Barclay Block, I tried to imagine what it would be like. Small, I supposed, since Rita lived alone — and was, in fact, the only person I'd ever known who did. Such an arrangement was new to me then, a future possibility that became more and more attractive the more I thought about it. The apartment would be quite small, yes, and half-dark all the time, with huge exotic plants dangling in all the windows, shedding a humid green light everywhere. The rooms smelled of coffee and black earth. The furniture was probably old, cleverly draped with throws in vivid geometrics. The hardwood floors gleamed and in one room (which one?) the ceiling was painted a throbbing bloody red. I thought that Rita and I could have coffee there just the two of us (my mother having conveniently disappeared) and she would tell me everything I needed to know. Why did Geoffrey hang himself, what happened to the baby, do you go out with men sometimes, do you think I'm pretty, do you think I'm smart? She could tell my future like a fortune.

We climbed a steep flight of stairs up to the second floor. The smell of baking bread rose up cheesy and moist from the Italian bakery below. I'd forgotten that my parents had lived here once too, until my mother said, "I always hated that smell, we lived in 3B," and pointed to a door on the left. I could not imagine anything at all about their apartment.

My mother knocked loudly on Rita's door. Further down another door opened and a woman in her housecoat leaned out into the hall, expecting somebody, I guess, or maybe just spying. "Oh, it's you. Hi," she said and ducked back inside.

My mother knocked again, and then once more.

"Maybe she's working," I offered.

"No, she's not. She definitely told me she was off today."

"Where can she be then?" I was pretty sure I could hear a radio going inside.

"How would I know?" my mother said angrily and sailed back down the hall.

Only once did I find my father and Rita alone in the house. I came home from Mary's late one Saturday afternoon and they were drinking rum at the kitchen table, with the record player turned up loud in the living room. They seemed neither surprised nor sorry to see me. There was something funny about Rita's eyes when she looked up at me though, a lazy softness, a shining, which I just naturally assumed to be an effect of the rum. She poured me a glass of 7Up and we sat around laying bets on the playoffs which were just starting, Montreal and St. Louis, until my mother came home from shopping. As it turned out, the Canadiens took the series four games straight that year and skated back to Montreal with the Stanley Cup.

Rita stayed for supper and then for the game. I went back to Mary's and then her father drove us downtown to the Junior A game at the arena. Rita was gone by the time I got home and I went straight to bed because I'd had one shot of rye in Lorne Puhalski's father's car in the arena parking lot and I was afraid my mother, who still liked to kiss me goodnight, would smell it.

They were arguing as they got ready for bed.

"She lost her son, Violet, and then her husband too," my father said, meaning Rita, making her sound innocent but careless, always losing things, people too. But he was defending her, and himself too, protecting her from some accusation, himself from some threat that I'd missed, something unfair.

"Well, I *know* that, Ted."

"Don't forget it then."

"That's no excuse for anything, you fool."

"I didn't say it was."

"Be quiet, she'll hear you," my mother said, meaning me.

CLUES

EVERY FRIDAY JUST AFTER LUNCH, Linda Anderson went out to their wheezing blue Chevy in the driveway next door and sat there honking for me — a ritual which irritated my mother marvelously and made me feel like I was going out on a heavy date. We were going grocery shopping.

Once in the car, I would admire Linda's new lilac skirt, multi-colored sandals, or glittering earring and brooch set. She made the jewelry herself from little kits she got every week through a special mail order club in the States. She was always wearing something new and flamboyant to, as she cheerfully put it, "perk myself up a bit. I know I'm plain." Even then I could see that this was true. Linda was one of those young women I've often seen since, on buses or trains, pale and rabbity-looking with slightly buck teeth and round eyes, baby-fine hair, light brown or dirty blonde depending on how you look at things. One of those young women destined to be always unhappy, unhealthy or alone.

In the Safeway store I pushed the cart while Linda joyfully loaded it up, tossing in items from either side, checking her list, flipping through the fistful of discount coupons we'd been dutifully clipping from magazines and newspapers all week. This did not take on the stingy penny-pinching quality it did when I was forced to go grocery shopping with my parents on Saturday. Then, my mother led the way, my father pushed the cart, which was invariably one of those balky ones with the wheels going in all directions at once, and I lagged along uselessly behind. My mother didn't even need a list. She bought exactly the same things every week. You could count on it.

The Safeway on Saturday was full of disgruntled men and hectic children. But on Fridays the shoppers were mostly women, moving smoothly and courteously through the aisles, sure of themselves, experts in their element.

Linda dropped her purchases one by one into the cart. Kraft Dinner, cream corn, brussels sprouts, dish soap. Gallons of milk. "Neil's a real milk-drinker."

Green beans. "Neil hates green beans but they're on sale."

Macaroni. "Neil just loves my macaroni and cheese."

I felt myself to be collecting these clues, learning everything there was to know about Neil Anderson and so, by extrapolation, about men in general. Neil, like all the other desirable men in the world, was swarthy and slim, brooding, sensitive and hard to please.

More items were checked off the list. Tomato soup. "It always comes in handy."

Fish for Friday. "We're not Catholic, but still, it's nice."

Cheese slices. "Last night I made this new casserole with sausage and cheese slices and was it ever good."

Linda was always trying out new products, new dishes. She had a whole shelf of cookbooks in her kitchen, from which she liked to read me recipes out loud: Apple-Ham Open-Facers, Inside-Out Ravioli, Lazy Day Lasagne. She prided herself on both her cooking and her shopping. Being seven years younger, I was immensely interested in the entire procedure, confident that this was one of the inevitable things which lay in store for me — shopping and cooking for my husband and our eventual children — they would all love everything I served them.

We waited at the meat counter while the butcher in his bloody apron sliced four chops off a big chunk of pork. The vertical blade whined through the flesh, silver teeth grinding on bone. The man in line behind us, wearing tinted glasses and a uniform of some kind, said, "That's just how it sounds when they cut the top of your head off to do an autopsy." Linda smiled and nodded, dropping the chops into the cart which I was already pushing away. Now the butcher was spearing slabs of dripping liver with a pointed wooden stick.

On the way to the checkout stand, we had to stop at the candy counter to pick up something for Neil, licorice pipes or jujubes or a chocolate-covered cherry. "I have to get him a little treat or he'll be mad at me," Linda explained coyly, making her husband sound like a spoiled child or maybe a snake she had managed to charm, but just barely.

The Andersons had moved into the house next door on the first of July, newly married, just come to Hastings from Newberry, a dumpy little town to the north. Jobs were easier to come by then and within the week, Neil was working at the same paper mill as my father.

In the beginning Linda came over to our house several times a week. She could sit at our kitchen table all afternoon just chatting and drinking coffee with my mother. We soon knew all about her.

Her maiden name was Jessop. Her family had been in Newberry for decades. They owned both the dry goods store and the funeral parlor now, though they'd started out with nothing just like everybody else. Linda was in the middle, with two older sisters and two younger brothers. There had been one older brother, Lance, but he was dead now, beaten to death outside the Newberry bar by a jealous husband from a neighboring town. The husband had then driven home, on a tractor no less, and killed his wife with a pitchfork. "As I see it," Linda said, "he knew he'd get caught so he figured he might as well finish the job."

Linda and Neil had been childhood sweethearts. "His family is basically no-count," she admitted. "Oh, don't tell him I said that, he'll kill me." As if I would. She was drawing me into a womanly conspiracy, lush with the promise of fat secrets and special knowledge.

But they were good at heart, the Andersons. In fact, one of Linda's brothers would soon be married to one of Neil's sisters. "It's a real family affair."

They were renting just until they could afford to buy a house in one of the new subdivisions. They planned to have three children and were getting busy on that right away. "I can't afford to wait too long," Linda confided. "Both my sisters were cut open for cancer when they weren't much older than me. So I suppose it'll get me too, in a few years."

Linda's life, past, present and future, was endlessly interesting to her, and to me too. But my mother wasn't much for socializing or sitting around gabbing all day, so, after the first few visits, she developed the habit of drifting inconspicuously back to the dishes, the dusting, or rolling up socks. Linda hardly seemed to notice her defection and I was flattered to think that it was really *my* company she sought in the first place.

Once, after Linda had finally gone home to start supper for Neil, my mother said viciously, "That girl's a feather-brain!" and threw the dish towel across the kitchen after her. "And don't you go getting any crazy ideas, young lady." I could not have said exactly what she meant — ideas about what? men, marriage, babies, cancer? — but I knew, grudgingly, that she had a point of some kind.

Linda had other stories besides her own — a repertoire of alarming gruesome tales which, for a time, I neither doubted nor forgot. But I didn't repeat them either. There was the one about the man who murdered his son and his dog with an axe. The woman found strangled in her car beside the Number One highway. The man who chopped up his wife and kept the parts in the freezer, all packaged up and labelled.

Such things happened all the time, in California, Paris,

Vancouver, Brazil, but they could happen to anyone anywhere. There was no reason to think that you would be spared. You could no longer know what to expect of people, especially men, in this crazy world. There were so many of them, all equally unpredictable. Most of the time there was no telling what they might do. According to Linda, the men were depraved savages who might run amok at any time and the women were helpless obvious victims, dying all over the place. The best and the worst of her stories were those in which the killers were *never caught*.

One afternoon Linda asked, "Did you hear about those kids?" casually stirring more sugar into her third cup of coffee. My mother was defrosting the fridge with pots of hot water.

"No," I said. My mother sat down at the table, wanting, I suppose, to hear the news in spite of herself.

Linda settled in to tell the story. "This couple took their four kids to an arts and crafts show at the community center. When they left, two of the kids, a boy and a girl, went on ahead. But they never got home. They found them the next day, strangled, side by side, in a field not far from the center."

"Here in Hastings?" I asked, for lack of any other response.

"Yes. Right here in Hastings."

My mother jumped up from the table, knocking her chair over backwards, and stomped out the door, muttering, "Garbage, garbage!" Which could have been either what she was going to do, put out the garbage, or her opinion of Linda, or both.

That night after supper I went through the newspaper page by page, hoping that no one would ask what I was looking for. On the second last page, I found the small headline, KIDS FOUND DEAD, above a half-inch story. Two children found dead in a schoolyard in Caracas, Venezuela. They'd been left at home alone and discovered missing when their parents came home the next day.

I was both disappointed and relieved. Linda, in her hurry to tell us something horrible that we didn't already know, got the story all wrong. She was looking for proof that she was justified in her cheerful expectation of tragedy. After this, there were many times when I suspected her of lying, trying to make me as frightened as she was. This did not immediately make me like her any less, although it probably should have and would now.

I was soon spending more time at Linda's house than she did at ours. My mother, I could see, had succeeded in making her feel, if not exactly unwelcome, then certainly unappreciated.

The Andersons' house was just the way ours had been before we renovated. We called them war-time houses. They were single storey squares with dugouts instead of basements, small cosy or cluttered rooms all opening off the kitchen, and wooden steps front and back.

When we were too hot and miserable to do anything else, Linda and I sat out on her front step in our shorts, watching the traffic and sipping pink lemonade till we felt pickled in it. Occasionally a carload of boys would slowly cruise by, whistling as we stretched and admired our legs in the sun. We were feeling like sleepy cats and ignored them.

My legs were a deep reddish-brown, so dark by August that my mother said, "You look like a little Indian." Linda was fair-skinned but neither burned nor tanned, remaining all summer long a marbled, bluish white. "Too much sun is bad for you anyway," she said. "It'll give you cancer." I didn't believe her and continued to cultivate my color. I couldn't help but notice that the blue veins in her thighs were beginning to bulge and break.

When it was cooler or raining, we sat inside, usually at their stylish new breakfast nook which Neil had built himself and Linda had wall-papered in a blue and orange pattern featuring teapots and coffee mugs.

32

While Linda talked, polished her salt and pepper shaker collection, or fussed and cooed over Twinky, the blue budgie in his cage by the window, I took careful note of everything in the house. The teapot clock, the ceramic Aunt Jemima canisters, the hot pot holders which read, "Don't Monkey With The Cook," the plastic placemats with kittens, roosters, or roses on them — she changed them once a week.

Every detail was important to me, an avenue into the esoteric intricacies of married life, a state of being which seemed to me then divinely blessed, glamorous, intimate but clean. I needed to know exactly how you achieved such a permanent and inviolable state of grace. As far as I was concerned, their perfect happiness was a foregone conclusion, stretching sanguinely out to embrace infinity. Any connection or resemblance between their marriage and that of my parents was remote, if it existed at all. It did not occur to me that either my parents had once been just like Linda and Neil or that Linda and Neil would one day be just like my parents, solidified and decidedly unromantic.

Linda, herself still quite convinced of the powerful magic of homemaking, was more than happy to answer my nosy questions. I was digging for information, especially about Neil and what it was like to live with a man.

"How do you make an omelette? What TV shows do you watch? Does Neil help with the dishes? How often do you vacuum? What time do you go to bed? Do you ever stay up all night? Which side of the bed do you sleep on?" The questions I was afraid to ask were the most important.

Their bedroom door stood proudly always open, displaying a dainty doll in the middle of the white chenille bedspread, her voluminous pink skirt spread around her in layers like a cake. At home the bedroom doors were always shut tight, a concession to privacy, shame, or not having made the bed yet.

One rainy afternoon Linda had the bright idea of rearranging the living room furniture to surprise Neil when he got home from the mill. The aqua-colored couch and chair with arms at least a foot wide were unwieldy but simple enough once we threw our weight into it. Before moving the TV set we had first to take down the dozens of photographs in different-sized filigree frames which completely covered its top. This was a lengthy procedure which involved the identification of every person in every picture, who took which shot, and what the special occasion was and at whose house it was held that year. Dismantling the china cabinet where Linda kept her salt and pepper shaker collection was even worse. She estimated the collection at two hundred pairs but it seemed more like eight or nine hundred to me, every set different, from cupids to corn cobs, from Santa and Mrs. Claus to Paul Bunyan and his blue ox, Babe. By the time Linda was finished fondling and explaining them, I was so bored, impatient and somehow embarrassed for her, that I went home, leaving her sprawled on the couch, sweating and self-satisfied.

The one thing we had not touched was Neil's gun collection. Arrayed in wooden racks against the wall, the smooth metal barrels were perfectly, endlessly, polished, cool to the touch even in this unbearable heat.

I did not go back for several days and when I did, found everything once again in its original position. Neil, obviously, had not been impressed. I was obscurely pleased, meanly imagining that he'd made her put it all back by herself. No one was going to push him around, least of all silly, fluffy Linda. It served her right. She could be so tiresome. Some days — mean, sulky days — I'd taken to wondering how Neil — quiet, sensitive, so handsome Neil — could even stand her. I was beginning to understand why she had no other friends. And if I was too young for her, as my mother repeatedly pointed out, then she was certainly too old for me.

I didn't spend all my time that summer with Linda. In fact, I never saw her on weekends and seldom in the evening.

Spending the day at home, I usually wanted to stay inside and read, but felt obligated to go out and suntan. I would spread myself out on a beach towel in the backyard, armed with baby oil, radio and a pitcher of water to sprinkle on intermittently, believing this would speed the tanning process. I was essentially bored and uncomfortable but lying there made me feel more normal, doing exactly what I supposed all the other girls my age were doing or wanting to.

On weekends I lay there by the honeysuckle hedge hoping that Neil Anderson would see me and want me and go back inside and holler at pale gabby Linda. Whenever I heard a sound from that direction, I couldn't open my eyes for fear it would or wouldn't be him.

I could not have said when I began to feel this way about Neil. It was all Linda's fault anyway, I reasoned. She had made him seem so desirable, so serious and important, so perfectly male, the only man worth having. How could I help myself? I no longer wanted to be like Linda. But I did want everything she had, including her house and her husband. Linda, I imagined, was the only obstacle which kept him from me. Now I fantasized about their divorce.

Evenings were usually spent with my best friend, Mary Yurick, who had a job in the kitchen of a nursing home downtown and so was not available to me during the day. I was not yet allowed to work and envied her mightily, foolishly brushing aside my mother's wise words: "You'll be working for the rest of your life — so what's your hurry?"

Mary and I passed the time at her house or mine, watching beauty pageants and variety shows on TV, playing Scrabble or poker, sipping lemon gin from her father's well-stocked liquor cabinet whenever her parents were out for the evening. When the night was too warm, too long, too inviting, we went out and we walked, restless and uneasily innocent.

We headed downtown, past those boring plump houses just like ours, with flowers, families and fat dogs in the yard. Downtown where the dangerous young men were hanging in restaurant doorways, draped potently over parking meters or the hoods of hot cars, watching the bright street where something might happen to jerk them awake, something electric and clarion, like a siren. We were already aware of their power but not yet of the need to protect ourselves from it. We thought we could become part of it, did not know yet of the danger, of how they would use it over and against us, never offering a share.

We browsed through the record store which was always open late and peeked through the glass doors of the Hastings Hotel bar, longing. Once there was a fight out in front, two men thumping bloodless and silent on the sidewalk. Once a young woman lay face down on the curb, stinking. But nothing could deter us. We walked the nights on a leash that summer, Mary and I, all dressed up and tingling, daring each other to be disgusted. The summer was almost over and we had wasted it.

Some evenings I stayed home and read, not wanting to know. Alone in the hot house, I curled up on the couch in my nightgown with a new novel and just one light on, feeling safe and relieved. All the screens were up, hoping to catch a breeze, and I could hear June bugs hitting against them, falling to the ground on their backs. From all up and down the block came voices, thin music, the hum of sprinklers and lawn mowers. Once in a while I could hear someone else's phone ringing faintly.

My parents were out in the yard cutting peonies and roses just as it grew dark, their voices young and strong in the twilight. Sometimes they sat out front in the lawn chairs, citronella candles smoking in a circle around them to keep the mosquitoes away. I wondered what Linda and Neil were doing, wished I had never met them, would never be like them. Wished I could stay home here forever, here where they did not draw blood, here where you knew exactly what they expected of you, here where my father was coming in through the door and putting his arms around me for no reason. Here where I wanted to cry.

Friday night the week before school started, Linda called and invited me over.

"Neil's gone out again, I'm all alone. We could make popcorn, I'll do your hair." She was begging.

I was hard-hearted. "No, I can't. I'm going out with Mary." I wanted to hurt her. I wanted her to know that I had better things to do and was nothing like her after all. It was Friday and I was feeling frisky, thinking of what I would wear, who we might see, how late I could stay downtown without pushing my mother over the edge.

Grocery shopping that afternoon, Linda had been careless and preoccupied, missing half the items on her list, spending her money instead with desperate extravagance on T-bone steaks, fresh asparagus tips, a precious can of lobster. Her dirty blonde hair was greasy and her out-of-style pedal-pushers were held together at the waist with a big safety pin. She perked up only once, just long enough to tell me the story of a marine in Michigan who had murdered his wife and three children and then turned the gun on himself.

"It was a real bloodbath. You can imagine," she muttered with grim satisfaction, fondling a sweet-smelling cantaloupe before tossing it into the cart. "All I really want is one of those little gadgets you make melon balls with."

I was barely listening, absent-mindedly examining the onions, not thinking of anything else in particular, but not allowing myself to be interested either. Linda, I had decided, no longer needed to be listened to. Her grisly gossip was merely her way of reassuring herself that things could be and probably would be worse. Everybody needs to be certain of something.

In my smug, soon-to-be-undermined adolescent superiority,

I pitied her. But I was shutting her off, cutting her out, moving glibly away. We could not do anything for each other anymore.

On the way home we took a detour downtown, cruising several times slowly past the Hastings Hotel so Linda could squint intently at the doorway, looking for clues. Neil Anderson, I knew from eavesdropping on my parents, was in trouble for drinking at work (this from my father) and sometimes stayed out all night without Linda (this from my mother who liked to keep track of things). I was interested but only mildly surprised. Linda was one of those women who expected the worst and got it. Neil was clever, sly and volatile, capable of anything.

Linda attempted to confide in me. "I just don't know what to do," she began and then stopped.

She tried again. "I just can't believe that Neil would — " I was holding my breath, afraid to look at her. What did she want from me anyway? She was older, married, she wasn't supposed to have problems anymore. I would not be drawn into her miseries. I would not talk about Neil behind his back anymore. It felt now like a betrayal or a shameful admission of helplessness.

Downtown that night Mary and I hung around the Exchange Café for a while, spending our allowances on chocolate milkshakes and chips and gravy, and then we gravitated wordlessly towards the Hastings Hotel. We perched on the wooden bench out front where the winos slumped in the sunshine and sometimes slept under newspapers at night. The police would be by in half an hour or so, telling us to move along. We sat there smoking cigarettes stolen from Mary's mother and talking, mostly about how easy it would be to sneak inside and have a beer. We were all dressed up, trying to look older in earrings and, despite the cooler nights, new white tank tops selected to show off our silky suntans. But we both knew we wouldn't try it, not yet.

The boarded-up bar door opened — someone had kicked in

the glass again — emitting a belch of boozy laughter and a country and western chorus.

Neil Anderson came out with his arm around the waist of a blonde woman wearing skin-tight slacks and white cowboy boots. She was quite stunning in an ornamental sort of way, smiling all-inclusively around her, proud of herself. Neil was just drunk enough to be expansive and flirtatious, not at all the way he was around the neighborhood, not at all the way Linda made him out to be. Neither of us had the grace or good sense to look guilty.

He came right up to me and threw his other arm around my neck, kissing the top of my head. "Hiya, honey!"

Mary was impressed. Neil patted through the pockets of his black leather jacket, as if looking for matches or a gun. Exposing a gleaming buck knife strapped to his belt, he produced a mickey of rye.

"For you, ladies!" he said and swaggered away.

The bottle, of course, was a bribe, so I wouldn't tell Linda. As if I would. I probably should have been indignant or afraid, but instead I was feeling privileged and ripe with our secret, winking and wanting to go with them. I was aching for adventure and convinced now that Neil, more than anyone, knew where to find it.

Neil Anderson was the first in a long line of those handsome charmingly doomed men who would inhabit my life for a time — those lovely lazy men who could get away with anything and I would never tell. For a few years anyway I thought I had it all figured out.

FROGS

VAL'S MOTHER ALWAYS TOLD HER, "You've got to kiss a lot of frogs before you find your prince."

In the hot summer, there were green frogs everywhere, looping around on people's front lawns, hopping across the sidewalk, into the street, getting run over. Val's mother chased them away from the front step with the broom, even though her grandmother, who was staying with them for the summer, said a frog coming into your house would bring you good luck.

When Val finally caught one, a tiny one no bigger than her thumbnail, she carried it into the kitchen cupped in her hands, where it fluttered and thumped away like a heart. She called the little frog Bob after her dad, who would be killed the next winter in a car crash on Highway 6 North. But nobody knew that yet. He rummaged around in his pockets and found her an empty matchbox to keep it in.

Her mother, who was at the stove just starting supper, said, "That's not a frog, it's a toad. You'll get warts." She didn't though, and whatever it was, it didn't last long in the matchbox.

"What's the difference between a frog and a toad?" is a very common question.

Frogs live in or near water, are slender with smooth moist skin and long hind legs which make them excellent jumpers. Toads, on the other hand, are stocky with short legs, hop rather than jump, and have rough dry skin with warts. They live away from water, in the woods, the garden, sometimes even the cellar.

After Simon moved out, Val's mother was relieved and worried both at once — relieved because she'd never liked Simon anyway, even though she'd only met him once, but worried too because she couldn't imagine what Val was going to do next.

In a letter, Val's mother writes, *You're thirty years old now, Val. You'd better get your act together.* Val knows that what she really means to say is, *Do what I want you to do.*

Val replies faithfully in that special tone she has created for her weekly letters home. Grammatical, stable and complacent, this voice makes everything she tells her mother sound harmless, round and slightly empty-headed. Val writes about the weather (which is just great), the gas bill (which is ridiculous), the cat (who is thriving), and the plants (which aren't). She doesn't mention Leonard, the man she has been seeing lately, because she knows her mother will like him already and there's no sense getting her hopes up. Her mother has never demanded the truth anyway, only something digestible with the least amount of difficulty. This, Val assumes, is the natural state of families.

When Val was promoted to Loans Officer at the bank, she got her own office, which is off in one corner, with glass walls on two sides. Whenever she feels claustrophobic, she opens the curtains so she can watch the tellers chatting with the customers over the sound of the computers, passing money endlessly from hand to hand. Val was a teller for five years before the promotion. Her new salary is substantial — they obviously want to hang onto her. She feels valuable and sometimes even important.

On Friday afternoon, once the after-work payday lineups have started to subside, Val straightens up her desk and then goes into the washroom to comb her hair. She splashes cold water on her face and neck, dabs on a little perfume, and admires her new haircut which frames her face with fine blonde curls like feathers.

It's almost time to lock up. Val is going for a beer after work with some of the other women. They do this every Friday. It usually means no supper, some dancing, and a quick buzz. They are working, always working, these women, and they like to get out on the weekend.

Annette Cosgrove is Val's favorite person at the bank. Annette is the youngest woman there, maybe twenty-two, pretty in a pale red rabbity sort of way, and very bright. She's only been at the bank for four months but Val doesn't expect she'll stay long — the good ones never do.

After work on Friday, Val and Annette walk down to the tavern together. They get a good table, close to the dance floor but not too close, and save some chairs for the other women who'll be along shortly, once they get Marsha balanced. They order a jug of draft beer. Annette pays, Val will get the next one.

The tavern is crowded, with men mostly, just having a casual after-work drink too. The men have pushed several tables together and their chairs are sticking out at all angles as more men come to join them, pulling up empty chairs from other tables and squeezing them in somehow.

The phone up front keeps ringing and the bartender keeps calling out names over the microphone. It's the women at home with the kids who are calling. Supper's ready. The men dribble out one by one. The women on the phone must be angry but Val isn't sure why.

By the time the band starts at eight, the tavern is beginning to fill up again. Val and her friends are still wearing their clothes from work, vivid summer dresses, high-heeled sandals, no nylons. This makes them more noticeable than most of the other women in the tavern and different men keep coming to their table, one at a time, grinning.

"Do you want to dance?"

Sometimes yes, sometimes no.

Marsha and Mary keep pointing out possibilities all over the tavern.

"Did you see John over there? Nice eyes."

"I think he's still married."

"No, they're split up now."

"Nice eyes."

Val knows they're trying to fix her up but she's not sure yet if she's broken.

Annette is talking about her husband, Mike, yelling into Val's right ear to make herself heard over the music. She's been married for six months. She calls him "Old Mike" and makes him sound like a dancing bear, comical but potentially dangerous. It's as though being married to him means she can finally tell other women what a fool he really is.

"Let me tell you three things," Annette says.

"Okay, what?" Val asks.

"Don't ever get married."

"And?"

"Don't even fall in love."

"And?"

"Kill the first person you fall in love with."

"Here's to you!" Val raises her glass to Annette's and they're laughing.

Across the table, Marsha and Mary, who are sisters, both twenty pounds overweight and always on a diet together, are talking about food.

Marsha says, "I don't believe in white sugar," and makes it sound like a fanatic fringe religion instead of a condiment.

Annette is still talking about Mike. She wants to sell the trailer and move to Vancouver but Old Mike won't hear of it.

Now they're all four talking about birth control, which is something they always talk about when they get together. They've all tried everything but nothing's perfect. Annette, as usual, is leading the conversation. It's as though she can't imagine a reason to remain silent, a subject that can't be companionably excavated for anyone who cares to listen. This is the sphere she functions best in — intimacy and confession. And confessions are meant to be reciprocated — otherwise what possible good can they be?

The waitress comes and clears the table, empties the ashtray, and tells Annette she can't put her feet up on the chairs like that.

Val orders another jug and feels a warm desire to give Annette what she wants — secrets, memories, probably a few tears too. Annette will accept whatever she is given, will nod, smile, encourage, support. She does not debate, question, or criticize. You can say anything to her.

By this time the odd drink is getting knocked over but the little round table is covered with blue terrycloth, elasticized so it fits tight. The spilt beer just foams up and is instantly absorbed.

It's almost last call. Everyone is dancing and clapping and singing along. The humid heat is getting to be like feathers in Val's throat.

Simon moved out on a Sunday in May. Val had never liked Sundays anyway, so later this would strike her as appropriate.

They were having, as they say, "an amicable separation," even though it had been Val's idea in the first place. It was still rather unclear to her as to why they were breaking up. Something important between them was gone, maybe it had been gone for a long time, maybe it was never there at all. They both knew this was true, they'd been talking about it for weeks — so much so that Val thought they were hardly even making sense anymore.

44

They spent the afternoon drinking a case of beer and gathering up Simon's things — typewriter, papers, clothes. Considering he'd lived in the apartment for a year and a half, he hadn't accumulated or contributed much.

It was not an altogether unpleasant day and they both admitted, laughing, to feeling relieved that it was all over now. They hadn't been sleeping together for weeks. Val pointed out that they hadn't been talking much either.

"We're getting along better right now than we have for months," she said. Simon had to agree.

Val made a simple supper, hamburgers and a tossed salad. She refused to think of this as their last meal together. Simon kept talking the whole time they were eating, clowning, telling jokes and silly stories. His long black hair kept falling in his eyes and his glasses were sliding down his nose. Val would automatically reach over and push them back into place.

"Wait, wait, I've got another one!" He waved the remains of his third hamburger at her. "What's red and green and goes two hundred miles an hour?"

"I don't know, what?"

"A frog in a blender!"

"Sorry I asked." She was laughing and rolling her eyes, picking bits of avocado out of the last of the salad.

When the beer was all gone, Simon put on his denim jacket, kissed Val and said, "I still love you, I guess I'll always love you. I'd better be going now."

Val said, "I love you too. You're my best friend."

Simon got into his truck and drove away. He was going to share a house with two other recently-single men. Val thought of them as "the walking wounded." Maybe he'd learn something.

Once Simon was gone, Val made herself a pot of tea, turned on the TV, settled herself in the big armchair and enjoyed herself immensely. Nothing in the room was changed — even the

45

stereo was hers — it was almost as though Simon had never been there at all. Val went to bed right after the news and slept better than she had for weeks.

The man Val is sleeping with now is Leonard DeVries, a lawyer. She has known him for a while because he deals at the bank. He's very handsome, all the women she works with say so, with deep blue eyes and short brown hair just beginning to go grey. He has a neat beard, brown streaked with red and grey. He's growing out all multi-colored. His chin could be any shape, maybe even receding or weak.

Leonard is always taking Val to places where she's never been before. They seem to spend all their time in restaurants and movie theaters and also in Leonard's new Porsche driving to and from these places.

Leonard's favorite restaurant is The Pines out on the highway just west of town. It's expensive and you have to be dressed up to feel comfortable eating there. The menu features every kind of seafood you could possibly imagine. They all know Leonard there and he always gets a table by the window so he can keep an eye on his car while they're eating. Outside in the parking lot people keep stopping to admire and touch it.

It is usually on these evenings spent at The Pines, two or three times a week, that Val and Leonard end up sleeping together. All that food and good service makes them both feel generous and lovable.

When they do sleep together, they sleep at Val's place. Leonard says, "This is a real home. I feel so comfortable here, I never want to leave." In the morning, he likes to putter around, watering the plants and playing with the cat, while Val puts on the coffee and gets ready for work.

At first Val thought Leonard was intelligent and very interesting. He seemed to know all kinds of things that she'd barely even thought about. He doesn't read books, only dozens of newspapers and magazines. He keeps up-to-date on everything. He is so calm that sometimes he makes Val nervous.

But already she thinks he's boring. He's always talking about himself without ever telling her anything. What she really wants to know is why he has been divorced twice, where are the wives, why did he never have children, why does he like her anyway, how much money does he really make?

Leonard is almost ten years older than Val, Simon is five years younger. She tries to make something of this, but can't.

After a few weeks of sleeping with Leonard, Val finds it is usually better to think about him than to actually be with him.

Leonard and Simon know each other, sort of, because they both belong to the tennis club. Val would like to keep them apart. If they spend too much time together, they might become like each other and then she would only be more confused.

One night over dinner at The Pines, Leonard says, "I ran into Simon downtown today, we had a few drinks together." Val finds it unsettling to think of them being together, having a good time, without her. She always thought she could control them. It has never occurred to her that they might do just as well without her.

The waitress materializes abruptly with their Greek salads and seems to be bouncing lightly on the balls of her feet which are strapped into a complicated arrangement of blue straps and gold buckles. Val studies them — she *is* bouncing.

Leonard digs in happily. Val sucks on her imported beer.

Already they are merging, then, Simon and Leonard, trespassing on each other. Their beards will grow out the same color, sandpaper on her chin. They will play tennis together on weekends. In later years they will adopt similar gestures, admire the same women, see the same movies, have backyard Sunday barbecues with bloody steak and pink lemonade. She will serve them vodka and tonic, frosted glasses sliding on the wooden tray, and they will smile: "Thanks, Val, you're a doll." They will start talking again as soon as her back is turned. They're sitting in plastic lawn chairs, wearing Bermuda shorts, crossing and uncrossing their hairy legs. They will touch her in all the same places, grow twin erections at the mere sight of her breasts. Boys will be boys.

The main course arrives discreetly. Leonard is having a steak, Val, prawns in garlic butter. Leonard is smearing sour cream all over his baked potato. One of the things she already hates about him is the way his jaw cracks when he's chewing.

"Did you talk about me?" she asks.

"No, I don't think we did."

This is worse, even worse. Oh, to be so civilized. Maybe they should have.

One of the good things about sleeping alone is that you can get up again after you've already gone to bed and there's nobody to ruffle the blankets and mumble, "What's the matter? Are you okay?"

Val, in her nightgown and Simon's old slippers, makes herself a cup of instant hot chocolate and a piece of brown toast. The fridge gurgles flatulently. She doesn't check to see how late it is. Early or late, there's no telling time now.

Val goes into the dark living room without turning the light on and stands by the window. She's not afraid of the dark anymore now that she understands about how you can die in the daytime too. In the half-light, her feet are like puddles on the hardwood floor. She hasn't bothered to wax the floor lately and there are Rorschach wine stains on one throw rug. Simon has been gone for three months now. Leonard is out of town on business but he'll be back tomorrow.

Behind Val's apartment building, there is a small nameless creek and by the light of the moon, which will be full soon, Val can see the water shining and moving. This makes her think she can hear it too.

Some of the things Val wants to think about are too depressing. The only way to approach them is to sneak up on them from behind. She has a sense of having made the one irrevocable mistake that will ruin the rest of her life. She tries to pass this off as some melodramatic trick of the moon, fails, and panics.

Someone is walking through the backyard of the building. Caught, guilty, Val lets the curtain fall shut. She is suspicious — of the late-night wanderer, of herself. Up to no good.

She thinks of this as her secret life.

Simon and Val had only known each other for a month when he moved into her apartment. The house he was living in had been sold and he had to move on the first of January. They didn't discuss it much (or enough, Val would think later) — it seemed only logical that he should move in with her. They had both lived with other people before.

They spent New Year's Eve alone in the apartment and celebrated with lobster and champagne at midnight. Simon ran out onto the balcony and hollered "Happy New Year!" at the street, which was gently filling up with snow.

They finished the champagne in bed. Simon brushed Val's hair away from her face and stroked her cheeks, whispering, "You're lovely, you're lovely," over and over again. He did this every night for a long time.

That May Val took a week's holiday and they rented a cabin at Hazel Lake. The cabin belonged to a fellow Simon worked with at the lumber yard. He'd taken a part-time job there to support himself for a few months while he worked on his second novel. His first had never been published which, Simon said now, was just as well. He was having some trouble with the second one though, and hadn't accomplished much during the past month. "Writer's void," he called it. They both hoped this week away would get the ball rolling again.

The road in was soft and muddy, it had rained off and on all week. Hazel Lake, when they came in sight of it, was grey and flat-looking, metallic. It was early in the season and all the other cabins were still boarded up. There was nobody else around.

The cabin was lopsided and weather-beaten, shedding flakes of paint. Val and Simon unloaded the truck in the rain — suitcases, fishing rods, typewriter, enough food, wine, and kerosene to last out the week. Inside, one large square room served as both kitchen and living area. There were two smaller rooms, curtained off — the bedroom and a storage room full of dry wood for the fireplace. The whole place smelled like wet wool.

Val and Simon were both awake for a long time the first night, lying in bed, holding hands, listening to the rain on the tin roof. Val was thinking that they were perfect here together, the way it should always be, could too, if only.

It rained every day, which was fine. Val was sleeping in late every morning, then fishing a little, walking by the lake, hugging herself against the rain. Frogs croaked around the lake all day long, a sign of more rain. Simon was always up early, writing, the sound of his typewriter coming to Val in her half-sleep, just like the rain on the roof. In the evenings, they played cribbage and backgammon in their bathrobes, drinking white wine out of coffee cups.

On Saturday night, their last night, they were reading in bed — Simon, the pages he'd written that day, and Val, an article on divorce in an old magazine. She said, "I think you and I are the only two people I know who haven't been married at least once. I'm glad you have no ex-wives hanging around any-where."

Which wasn't exactly what she meant to say but was as good a way as any to open the discussion, which was an ongoing one they'd been having for several weeks now — this one was only a sample — and it wasn't over yet.

Simon didn't even hesitate, he jumped right in. "I'll never get married, I'll never have kids, I've always known that."

"But you didn't know me before."

"It doesn't make any difference."

"But what about me?"

"I love you. I don't need to marry you to prove it."

"What about what I want? Doesn't that matter to you?"

"I'm sorry, I guess I'll never change."

They went on for an hour at least, back and forth, back and forth, until Val couldn't believe she was saying any of this anyway and she was sobbing and hitting Simon weakly in the chest.

Simon held her until she stopped crying, then got up and went into the other room. He came back with a towel and a pot of warm water and gently washed her face.

They began to make love, slowly, carefully. Val moved to get up for her diaphragm.

Simon said, "You don't have to."

"What if I get pregnant?"

"It doesn't matter."

But nothing came of it. Val was mostly relieved. How could they have been so foolish? They weren't talking about marriage and babies much anymore anyway. Just as well.

Simon has a new job waiting on tables part-time at the tavern, weekends mostly, filling in for the regular staff. Val already knows this before she goes down on Friday with the girls. Annette was in with her husband the night before and she told Val.

They sit in Simon's section because that's where they always sit — it's closer to the band.

Val is so glad to see Simon that at first she talks even more than Annette and dances with everyone who asks her. Simon is an extremely efficient waiter and they're all giving him big tips which embarrasses everyone, but not in a bad way. Val notices that he's wearing a new plaid shirt and he's had his beard trimmed.

While the band is taking a break, Annette tells Val that Mike is pushing her to get pregnant.

"I'd never have a baby in this God-forsaken town," Annette declares. Marsha and Mary, who already have families, don't say anything. Val envies Annette even though she knows she's unhappy.

She's watching Simon all the time but he's so busy he doesn't have time to talk to her. It's been a hard day, Marsha never did balance, and Val is very tired. She knows she should go home early but she'd rather stick around and see what happens.

When the band has finished playing, complete with two ragged encores, and the bar is closed for the night, Val expects that Simon will come and sit down with her. But he leans up against the bar instead, counting his tips and chatting with the bartender.

On her way out, Val asks him if he needs a ride home but he says, "No thanks, I've got the truck." Some young girl with dark curly hair and a pretty mauve sweater has been hanging around him all night and she's still there, waiting.

Simon is coming over for coffee. It's already quite late, Val was getting ready for bed when he called but she didn't even think of telling him not to come. She puts the kettle on and debates with herself about getting dressed again. She puts a record on and stays in her housecoat.

When Simon arrives, the cat immediately jumps into his lap and goes to sleep, purring. Val tries not to see this as significant.

They are both uncomfortable, obviously, and Val finds this disappointing. Simon tells her about his novel, which is nearly done now. He's going back out to the cabin for a week to finish it. It's almost the end of September, there won't be anybody else around.

Val says, "What about your job at the tavern?"

"Things are pretty slow right now, they won't need me again for a couple of weeks."

Val says, "How come you never talk to me when I'm there with Annette? Why can't we be friends?" She knows that questions can be dangerous. They make you vulnerable to the answers, which are uncontrollable. She wants to offer Simon some more coffee but she wants him to leave too. She has to go to work in the morning.

"I don't want to be your friend. Will you come to the cabin with me?"

Val gets up and refills their cups. She's trying to think of an answer, she doesn't know what she wants to say.

Simon says, "I want to get married someday."

It is not a question.

"I won't hold you to that."

"Yes you will."

CRIMES OF PASSION

JACK MARSH DIDN'T LIKE PARTIES much but he went to this
one anyway because he'd been out of town, working up in
Edmonton, for two weeks and because Benjamin Kozak was his
best friend. When he got to Ben's, late, everyone was in the
living room dancing, drinks in hands, in front of the picture
window. Most of the dancers were women. Leaping and
bright-colored, their reflections were like flames in the glass.
Beyond them, outside, it was snowing thickly. The snowflakes
were like moths around the streetlights.

Ben's new house wasn't finished yet and, without curtains,
baseboards or carpet, the room looked raw. Jack thought Ben
would never get the place finished now that his wife, Carol,
had left him. Jack thought of Ben as a soft, slow-moving man
whom Carol, with her loud voice, plush body and gourmet
cooking, had quite consciously spoiled, mastered, and then
abandoned. Now Ben was always giving parties, filling up the
unfinished house with young women and beer.

Ben, who seemed to be dancing with all the women at once,
caught sight of Jack and wiggled his beer bottle at him, gesturing
towards the kitchen.

Jack found Emily Lipton in the kitchen.

He supposed it was inevitable that they would keep meeting
like this, at parties, on the street, in the grocery store, for years
to come. They'd been together, in one form or another, for
three years and he assumed their lives would always be
connected somehow, if only by coincidence. Even when they'd

first split up two months ago, he didn't think, Now I'll never see her again. Aurora was a small town and they had all the same friends and it never occurred to him that one or the other of them might move away someday. Jack thought they'd be good friends when they were old.

Emily stood with her back to him, looking out the window. Jack couldn't tell if she was trying to see out or was merely admiring her face in the glass. He knew that her new lover, Tom, lived right across the back lane. Carol had told him.

He said, "Carol told me you'd be here."

Without turning, Emily said, "She told me you'd be here too."

Jack helped himself to a handful of pretzels and a slippery cocktail wiener. On the counter, there were also ripple chips, a bag of Oreo cookies, and a green tin of dill chip dip. He couldn't help thinking that if Carol was still around, they'd all be having yogurt dip with chilled fresh vegetables, camembert and brie, liverwurst and lox. Carol used to give great parties. People just naturally gravitated around her and she thrived on it. If Carol was still around, the party would be in the kitchen. She was always cooking something that smelled good and would feed everybody. Along with the food, Carol dispensed advice, recipes, back-rubs and the perfect wine. She was always the center of everything. The house organized itself around her whether she was there or not. And when she wasn't there, Jack thought, everyone seemed to be expecting her to arrive any minute now.

"How is Carol these days?" he asked. He and Emily always talked about Carol. She was the buffer zone between them. Jack leaned against the stove.

"Doing very well," Emily said. "She was sorry she couldn't make it tonight but she thought it was too soon."

Carol Kozak was Emily's best friend. When she left Ben three weeks ago, Carol had moved in with Emily temporarily.

Whenever Jack and Ben talked about being left (which was seldom), they were both always looking for someone else to blame. Usually Ben blamed Emily and Jack blamed Carol, but sometimes they switched it around.

Emily finally turned to face Jack. She was eating a banana.

"You're eating a banana."

She looked down at it.

"Emily, I just don't understand you."

She was still looking at it.

"You never ate bananas when you were with me. Emily, you *hate* bananas." This was some kind of accusation. They were always accusing each other of something.

"Oh Jack. People change, you know."

"Well, I haven't." He was proud of this, proud to think that his life was just the same without her. He saw no reason to change. He thought this proved something but he hadn't figured out what yet.

Emily was angry now. She said, "Jack, this is ridiculous," and threw the banana peel in the sink. But then she was already smiling at him again.

Her moods were changing too quickly, shifting like sand so Jack couldn't keep track of them. Jack had no patience with moods, his own or other people's. He admired consistency, not eccentricity, which made him uncomfortable because he could never be sure what would happen next. This was something new about Emily too. He used to know exactly how she'd react to anything he might choose to say. He liked to think he'd never intentionally used this to hurt her. Jack thought of himself as a noble man and he wondered why they couldn't have a casual conversation anymore. He thought of the last few months they'd been together and how every day there'd been something else, another emotional complication, one more layer to add to the pile. Now there were more things they *couldn't* talk about than things they could.

He stepped towards her, reaching awkwardly across and behind her, feeling for the light switch. This was the closest together they'd been since she left him and he regretted it instantly. He was afraid she'd touch him. Emily had always been the one to touch first, kiss first, touch again, rubbing the same spot on his back until it went numb. Jack was afraid that if she touched him now, even accidentally, he would pull away and she would be hurt. He thought he didn't want to hurt her. But she didn't touch him.

Jack flipped on the overhead light and retreated back to the stove. They'd been talking in the dark and suddenly it had reminded him of being in bed with Emily and she always wanted to talk before they went to sleep and he would be too tired and she would tease him, saying she'd had a deprived childhood because she was an only child and she had no sisters to talk to in the dark. Sometimes she was laughing and petting him while she talked. But he would fall asleep anyway, sometimes right in the middle of a sentence, and then she would be mad and go sit in the living room and smoke cigarettes for an hour or two. Once she went out for a walk at three in the morning even though she was afraid of the dark, but Jack was sleeping and he never knew until she told him and then she never did it again.

The fluorescent light was comforting. Jack looked at Emily more closely. She was sipping her beer and concentrating on the music or something else. She would never again, Jack realized, make things easy for him. She was wearing a baggy cream-colored blouse and a long billowing skirt, dark blue patterned with intricate flowers and leaves, made of that puckered cotton that always made Jack think of incense and wheat germ. She used to wear plaid shirts and jeans. Whenever Jack thought of Emily, she was wearing a red plaid shirt and faded jeans.

Sometimes he used to tell her how much he admired women

who looked like *real* women. Emily never seemed to know what he was talking about so then he would point out certain women on the street as examples. These women were always wearing summer dresses, gold earrings, sheer nylons, and high-heeled sandals that made their calf muscles stand out like plums. Sometimes Jack imagined how it would feel to have a woman like that walking beside him, her perfume coming to him in subtle waves, her nylons rustling as her high-heels clicked on the concrete. But really Jack thought these women were too good for him. They were queens; Emily and most women were what he called "utility grade." This second group was much larger than the first. Queens were women he wanted but was afraid of; utility grades were women he didn't want very badly but they were, he thought, friendly, manageable and grateful.

Jack used to say, "Emily, I want a real woman, a feminine woman. You could be one if you tried." He didn't understand why this made her so mad. He meant it as encouragement, not insult. Emily seemed so unsure of herself, of how she wanted to be — he figured she was just waiting to be shown. He thought of Emily as the kind of person who was always being given advice just because she always looked like she was asking for it, whether she was or not. This still felt true.

Now it seemed like Emily was still wanting him to have an opinion of her. The long skirt clung to her thighs; her arms and neck were naked. Maybe now she wanted him to admire her from afar.

It had only been two months but Emily's hair looked much longer, falling loose and tangled down her back like dark vines. Jack had always liked it long (it had been that way when they first met) so he said, "I like your hair. New clothes too?"

"Yes, and I made the skirt myself." Emily turned half around to make the skirt spin out and then drape around her legs.

Jack fished around in the fridge and came up with two more cold beer. He opened them and handed one to Emily, resisting the urge to point out the fact that she'd never sewed when they were together. He pictured her hunched over the sewing machine, pins in her mouth and yellow threads in her hair, teeth clenching and unclenching as she jammed the fabric through. This, he remembered, had something to do with her childhood too. Emily and her mother, Fern, who could sew everything perfectly, were always fighting about it. There was some long, involved and emotional story about a brown jumper that he couldn't remember anymore.

Jack didn't know what to make of Emily's parents, Mr. and Mrs. Lipton. The summer they came from Ontario to visit Emily, it was hot every day for two weeks and Mrs. Lipton sat out in the back yard with her feet in a bucket of cold water because her ankles were swelling with the heat. Arthur Lipton was just quiet and nervous all the time. Emily was always telling Jack how wonderful her parents were, but when they were all together, they never seemed to get along. Jack couldn't understand any of this.

He thought his own parents were perfect. They lived in Edmonton and were quite well off. Mr. Marsh was a lawyer and owned three large apartment buildings. Jack couldn't understand why Mr. and Mrs. Lipton, who certainly weren't rich, were always spoiling Emily even though she'd been away from home, living in Alberta, for five years. They kept sending her money and big boxes filled with fancy towels, canned lobster and electric appliances. Jack's parents never gave him money or presents anymore, except at Christmas. They'd brought him up to be an independent man. Whenever he had to work up in Edmonton, he stayed at their house but he paid daily room and board and did his own ironing. Mr. and Mrs. Marsh didn't like Emily and their opinion was important to Jack.

Now he said, "It's a pretty skirt, yes, very nice," but he thought it didn't suit her.

A round woman in black satin pants walked between them.

People kept coming into the kitchen like this, getting more beer, more pretzels, or just passing through on their way to the bathroom. It was, Jack thought, like being on a train and he and Emily were talking only because they'd happened to get on at the same stop.

It wasn't that Jack wanted Emily back. It was just that he didn't want her to change. He wanted her to be always the way she had been when they were together. He didn't want to think of her going out and buying bananas, yards of blue cotton, a sewing machine, all these things that had nothing to do with him. The changes in Emily made him think the woman he'd known somehow wasn't true anymore, never had been. He couldn't decide which Emily was the real one and he still needed to know. Sometimes he thought she'd been putting on an act for three years but other times he thought she was putting on an act now. There was no way of knowing her anymore.

"How does Carol like her new job?" Jack asked. Carol was always starting a new job. This one was with a travel agent. The last one had been with a firm of lawyers and the one before that with a real estate agency. Carol's jobs never lasted more than six months. She always quit. Jack thought she was irresponsible, not exactly shiftless, but sadly careless in shaping her life. He and Emily used to argue about Carol. He would say Carol was a bad influence and then Emily would defend her fiercely, ending lamely with, "Well, she's my best friend, you know." To which Jack would reply, "But that doesn't make her a good person." He thought this was obvious but sometimes it made Emily cry.

Jack's opinion of Carol, however, didn't stop him from confiding in her now and pumping her for information about Emily. He would inspect and analyze his feelings out loud for Carol, knowing full well that she would, in turn, relay them on to Emily. Once he said to Carol, "If she'd given me half a chance, I might have married her." Later Carol said that Emily, when she heard this, said, "What's that supposed to mean?"

Emily was looking out the window again. It irritated Jack that she wasn't paying attention to him, even though what he was saying wasn't really important at all. He wondered if she'd always had this habit of drifting in and out of conversation with him.

"How does Carol like her new job?" he asked again.

Ben came into the kitchen for another beer. He was rumpled and damp from the dancing. "Does Carol have a new job?" he asked.

"She's working for a travel agent now," Jack said.

"She thinks this job will take her somewhere," Emily said.

"She always thinks that," Ben said gloomily. "What she can't understand is that no job and nobody will take her anywhere. She just has to get there all by herself like the rest of us."

Jack hated this new philosophical tone of Ben's. He was seeing a psychologist once a week and sounding more and more profound after each visit, more serenely sad, more proud of being so hurt. Jack believed that there are some things that should never be said out loud because they give too much away.

Ben had his back to them as he rummaged in the fridge. Emily raised her eyebrows at Jack who instantly resented her attempt at conspiracy. She was always doing this, drawing people to her with promises of intimacy and secrets. She did this to everyone, especially other women. Jack thought she had no sense of discrimination.

When they used to go grocery shopping together on Saturday mornings, Emily was always stopping to say, "Hello, how are you?" to somebody. These other shoppers were mostly women, Emily's own age or older. They almost always had something attached to them: shopping carts, strollers, shy husbands, assorted children. One woman, her name was Betty Champagne, kept her little boy on a leash. She said he was hyperactive. Another woman, Laurie Dorion, was pregnant with her fourth child. She always said, loudly, "I'll sure be glad to drop this thing. Never trust an IUD or a man either." Laurie had red hair and was always wearing a green sunsuit. She looked like an olive. Jack would wait beside the cart, sighing and folding and unfolding his arms, while Emily conducted these capsule conversations between the Corn Flakes and the Kotex, whispering and gossiping and making lunch dates.

Now Jack, by way of refusing Emily's invitation to take a side, said "Oh, you know Carol."

"Where is she tonight?" Ben asked, emerging from the fridge.
"I don't know."

Jack could see that Emily was still a lousy liar and he thought it served her right to be uncomfortable. She'd changed everything for all of them. Once they'd all been friends together, he and Emily, Carol and Ben. But now they were all sleeping in different camps. He was sleeping alone, Ben was sleeping around, Carol was sleeping on Emily's couch, and Emily was sleeping with Tom. Carol said Tom had a waterbed.

A sharp-breasted girl in a pink sweater came into the kitchen and jiggled all around Ben until he went back into the living room to dance with her some more. As he disappeared again into the music, Ben winked back at Jack who raised an eyebrow at Emily who smiled harmlessly at the fridge and said, "Her name's Marlene."

Somebody turned up the music and Jack could see more dancers galloping around the living room. Everybody seemed to be wearing fewer clothes.

Jack turned back to Emily and looked out the window with her. Tom's house was all in darkness.

"He's not there," Jack said.
"I know."
"Where is he?"
"I don't know."

Emily had been seeing Tom for just over a month. Carol kept Jack informed. Carol thought Emily and Tom were perfect for each other.

Emily and Jack had never talked about Tom but Emily had a clever way of slipping in his name at random moments of conversation. Jack never knew if she did this to hurt him or to assure him that she was all right now. He also never knew which way it made him feel.

Jack knew Tom to see him but that was all. Tom was an accountant and that meant he was always wearing a suit — brown, grey, blue, a black one once, with color-coordinated ties, shirts, and shoes. Although Jack expected that women should just naturally spend all their money on clothes, he was suspicious of men who might be doing the same thing. But Tom drove an old yellow pickup truck and Jack liked the truck.

"How are things with you and Tom?" It seemed all right to ask this question but Emily looked surprised.

Carol said Tom was good to Emily. There was some suggestion of a drinking problem but Tom was trying to get on top of it. Carol said one time Tom was in a car accident while he was out with an older woman named Joan. Tom was drunk and he drove off the road and into a tree. They walked six miles home on the highway because Tom was afraid the police would find him. Joan was only wearing summer sandals and Tom took off his mitts and put them on her feet. Carol said, "Some women are just never prepared for anything." Carol said Emily went back with Tom the next day to help pull the truck out of the ditch. And then she went with him to the police station and told them he'd hit a patch of glare ice and missed the corner.

"Good, we're really good," Emily said. "We're talking about taking a trip to Mexico. I applied for my passport already. Tom's been there twice before, he has friends there now, and he says I'll just love it."

That wasn't what Jack was asking.

Emily went on. "He's color-blind, you know. And when we go shopping for things for the trip, he's always hollering across the store at me to come and tell him the colors of everything. He laughs about it but I always think that even when I do tell him a shirt is brown, he still doesn't know what I mean. He'll never be able to see what we see."

Jack said, "I can see your car at his house from my back window." Jack lived just around the corner, half a block down. "Sometimes I drive by that way just to see if you're there. And then I'm disappointed if you are and if you're not."

Afterwards, Jack would try and remember how many beer he'd had because he would think that he had to be at least half drunk to admit such a thing.

Emily said, "One night at Tom's I couldn't sleep, I don't like waterbeds, and I was just lying there watching car lights on the ceiling. I sat up to look out and it was your car going by."

In a while, when Emily went to the closet for her coat, Jack went too.

She said, "You don't have to do this anymore."

"What?"

"Leave when I do."

"But I want to."

"All right then."

Jack realized that they'd missed the whole party. They'd always been this way at parties. Emily used to accuse him of never having figured out how to have a good time.

He waited outside on the porch while Emily put on her boots and scarf. Tom's house was still dark. The snow was so heavy it made the darkness look white.

When Emily came out, Jack said, "He's still not there."

Emily said, "I thought he'd be home by now."

Jack was watching the snow fall on her dark hair. He would have given her a ride home but she didn't ask. There had been something earlier about her car getting a new muffler. He knew she was afraid of the dark but there she was, smiling and waving and walking away from him anyway, and he was already feeling better. In the morning he would go skiing.

NOTES FOR A TRAVELOGUE

IT'S RAINING THE MORNING we pull out of town. We stop at the grocery store to buy juice and fruit for the first day of our trip. The usual Saturday shoppers haven't been put off by the weather. Husbands shrug their jackets up over their heads and run recklessly toward their cars, aiming themselves with keys held outstretched in one hand. Mothers scoop up their babies like footballs and jog across the street to the cars which are now ready for them, doors open, motors running.

We drive all day, passing through the rain and out into the sunshine. Actually, my husband Grant does the driving and I do the passengering. At first I feel guilty about not even offering to take a turn at the wheel, but what's the point? It's his car and he never lets me drive it far anyway. Just as well. Whenever I'm behind the wheel and he's there beside me, the car sputters ominously, convulses, jerks, stalls. My feet get tangled in the floor mat. Grant just sighs and sweats.

We've never had a holiday together before, even though we've been married for nearly two years now. Grant usually goes off alone while I stay behind, patient, understanding, watching for postcards and drawing red and blue felt-pen lines on the map he leaves me. He once admitted that he likes to think of me alone in the house with nothing to do but wait for him to come back home. I didn't contradict him. We have no children.

Some people have a baby to try and keep their marriage together. Other people buy a new house, build a rumpus room in the basement, put blue wallpaper up in the bathroom, buy a pair of his and hers snowmobiles. We're going on a week's holiday together.

The landscape we pass through is all new to me and I discover that cactus and rattlesnakes do grow in this country after all. Some teacher years ago in public school told me it could never happen here. My husband smiles at me in smug congratulation — I've finally figured out what he, of course, has known for years.

Once it gets dark, we pull into the first campground we come to, breaking away from the hypnotic bracelet of bright tourist towns strung up and down both sides of the highway. The place feels large and vacant as we pitch our tiny tent in the dark. Waving the flashlight around and shivering, I know I'm not being much help, but if Grant is annoyed, at least he doesn't say anything. Maybe I'm being too hard on him.

Morning reveals a white Winnebago squatting just down the way, fat with sleeping strangers. There seems to be ten or twelve of them, with interchangeable heads, emerging one by one in various states of half-dress. The children race down to the lake in a pack while the adults put the coffee on. Then they holler blindly back and forth at each other through the tree cover — warnings, discoveries, the breakfast menu. While I'm waiting my turn in the fibreglass outhouse, a white poodle licks amiably at my ankles. Grant pumps up the Coleman stove and breaks eggs seriously into a metal bowl.

We continue driving west. Fruit stands sprout up lopsided on both sides of the highway. The lakes here are slender and smooth, like legs, and the hills are lumpy, in multiple shades of burnt-out brown.

Grant would drive all day without stopping, I think, even though we began this trip determined to take our time, dispense with schedules (I didn't even bring my wristwatch) and dabble in the countryside as we went along. When I ask though, we can stop for photographs, lunch, a Coke, a toilet. While he waits for me, Grant kicks all four tires to check the pressure and picks dead bugs off the headlights.

For the last fifty miles there are cars on all sides of us, gathering us up, willing or not, into their desperate push onward, forward, ever forward, lemmings to the sea. The line of cars, four abreast in the rain, is like a train, unable to travel anywhere but on this track on which it's been set down.

We take the early evening ferry across the strait. The vibrating drone of the engines overpowers the motion of the water below us. I, who have never been on a ferry before, marvel at the seasoned sea commuters who space themselves courteously along the olive green benches, sip coffee, read the paper, play solitaire and hearts as if nothing is happening. Their kids and their cars are all waiting faithfully on the far shore. The boat pulls its way through the black water and I stand out on the deck till I'm soaked. This amuses Grant who hugs me pleasantly and leads me back inside.

We set up our camp that night in the middle of a twilight cedar forest. Grant scrounges around for dry wood and manages to build a respectable fire. We drag two stumps up as close to the flames as we can bear. Through the smell of smoking cedar, Grant with shining eyes says, "I don't know what it is about campfires, but they sure are hard to take sometimes."

No matter what happens next, we will always have this. No matter what I do, my husband, it seems, won't quite assume the villain's role the way I think he should.

We spend the next day exploring the forest, after discovering that all the edges of the ocean are owned now, and cannot be reached by the uninitiated. We cannot get down to the sea and content ourselves instead with admiring the rotund trees, moss dangling like green sleeves from their branches. The trees at home are skinny and vicious — they creak and come down in the wind, smashing windows, high wires and car roofs.

It's October and there's nobody else around. The spongy ground is quilted with maple leaves. It's hard to tell when the rain has stopped because the trees still spit down water like bird droppings when we brush accidentally up against them. We hold hands without thinking.

I've never spent seven straight days and nights with my husband before and I'm not sure yet that I like it much. Here there aren't the normal spaces furnished by his going off to work every day, by my going out to the grocery store or for a Sunday afternoon stroll with my friends and their babies, by my getting into the bathtub before bed and lolling around till I'm all wrinkled, all relaxed. Here there's no routine, here we have nothing to go on.

I don't think Grant wants to get rid of me exactly, but I sense him expecting something from me, a suggestion, a decision, a show of independence.

I guess I'm supposed to say,

"Come back for me in an hour or two, I'm just going to jaunt up this little mountain here."

Or,

"Come back for me in a year or two, I'm just going to fly up to Baffin Island and find myself."

But even when we go into town (Blue Hills, it's called) to pick up more eggs, some back bacon, milk, a green pepper, I trail around the grocery store behind him, afraid somehow of letting him out of my sight. Afraid for him or afraid for me? I don't know. If I told him this fear, he would say,

"Sharon, you're neurotic."

And I would say,

"No, I'm not, I'm not, I am *not* neurotic."

And he would say,

"Now you're getting hysterical."

My husband thinks I'm always on the verge of something —
hysteria, neurosis, tears, breaking down. He calls me "the wife"
when he thinks I'm not listening.

Late the next evening, we take a drive through the town of
Blue Hills, sucking on the ice cream cones we waited in line
to get and speculating about the lives of the strangers we see
framed by their yellow-lit windows, caught in suspended
animation with the curtains still open as we cruise through the
rain like spies.

The main street of Blue Hills has all the shops and businesses
down the west side, the strait on the east. Ragged wooden
docks poke into the water like tongues. There are lights further
out, another island. I think I see two people on the very end
of the longest dock, dangling their feet in the water, but then
again they may be only shadows.

I'm convinced that our extended silence is the comfortable
kind common to marriage until Grant says,

"This isn't working out. Let's head for home in the morning."

This is something I already know, but not something I want
to hear. I have to agree with him though.

We decide to spend our last night in the only motel in Blue
Hills — it is, in fact, named "The Only Motel" in blue and
white neon. Grant will not admit that he enjoys the idea —
maybe he doesn't, who knows? He goes through the whole
procedure of checking in, unlocking the room, dragging our
wet packs and tent inside, as if it were some final, shameful
concession to weakness, as if being in the motel instead of the
tent proves we just aren't strong enough to suffer enough after
all. I, for one, am glad to be here. I think my socks were
starting to mildew.

I've stayed in a motel with my husband once before and
already know there is nothing intrinsically erotic about motel
rooms. We go to bed early and watch colored TV. Grant keeps

jumping up to fiddle with the fine tuning and then falls asleep while the news is on. The sheets and pillowcases are yellowed and smell reassuringly of industrial strength laundry soap.

In the miniature bathroom there are many little bars of odourless soap, glasses in white paper bags, enough gold towels for ten people, and a strip of paper across the toilet seat that reads, "For Your Protection." In the morning I shower first and the water runs cold on Grant. He is an unlucky person.

I suppose we will stay together a while yet, my husband and I. But the end is inevitable, if only because he thinks so. He wants the end to be graceful and friendly, generous. He has his fantasies too — I can see that now. I suspect though, that we will hang onto each other until the alternatives have all been tried and the complications have set in. For now though it is simple. But Grant will never let me walk away feeling broken, self-righteous and sad. He will not let me sacrifice myself or anything else for this love, he wants me to be strong. He wants me to walk away from him silently, with a faraway but pleasant philosophical look in my eye.

Driving home will take longer than leaving. Anxious to arrive, I will pass the hours wondering how much mail is waiting for us, conjuring the sheets, tablecloth, drapes, new carpet, cat purring deep back in her throat like a pigeon, everything occurring and recurring in safe clean patterns. Grant will drive on steadily through the rain.

When we finally get there and the door is unlocked and we are inside, I will say,

"Why did we come home so soon? There's nothing for us here."

Wanting only for my husband to tell me that there is. But he, being a clumsy liar, will say,

"I hate to see you disappointed, but I knew you would be, Sharon."

I cannot find the energy to unpack, will rummage uselessly around in my pack while the cat winds herself around me in an excess of emotion. Without water for a week, the plants have all gone dead and brown on the ends.

This is not unpleasant because I'm already starting to know what I'm going to do.

THE LONG WAY HOME

MARY PHONED RUTH ONE SATURDAY early in June. It was two in the morning Ruth's time in Alberta, four o'clock Mary's time in Ontario.

Once Ruth came awake and determined that no one had died, Mary said she had two weeks' holiday starting next Monday and would be taking the train to Calgary to be matron of honor at her cousin's wedding. She wanted to get a bus out from Calgary and spend one night in Aurora with Ruth. So they made arrangements for a week from Wednesday.

Then they talked about their parents, other relatives, mutual friends, anybody they could think of. According to Mary, everyone back in Hastings was fine, just fine, or at least the same, still the same. The dramatic crises which had fuelled their high school years had, it seemed, mysteriously dried up as they all grew older. Ruth figured this must be either because they were all too busy now and weren't paying attention, or because those destined for early death, suicide attempts, and botched abortions had already fulfilled their fates, leaving the rest of them to muddle along unspectacularly. They didn't talk much about themselves because they hadn't seen each other for five years, not since Ruth left Hastings and moved away to Alberta.

Ruth described her apartment in Aurora and Mary described their new house on Elmwood Crescent so they could picture each other while they talked. Ruth was in the big corner chair in the dark living room, curled up naked inside the afghan her mother had just sent for her twenty-seventh birthday. The chair was brown and the afghan was every possible shade of blue. Mary said she was sitting at the kitchen table in her bathrobe, smoking low-tar cigarettes and drinking cocoa because she couldn't sleep. The bathrobe was green and the major appliances were harvest gold.

Ruth's new lover, Steve Schroeder, came out of the bedroom and splashed around in the kitchen getting a glass of ice water. The fridge light came on, milky blue on the ceiling. Mary said David was upstairs asleep, had been for hours, Lee-Ann too. David Barnes, Mary's husband, used to work at the grain elevator in Hastings but he'd quit last September to go to university. Now he was in first-year Psychology. Mary was supporting the family now, working for a real estate firm where she was always getting promotions, bonuses and complimentary steak dinners for two because she sold so many houses.

Ruth had only met David once and then just long enough to discover that he was a chronic and vicious Monopoly player. She imagined him now, dreaming of Boardwalk and Park Place, twitching. She'd never seen Lee-Ann, their three-year-old daughter, and tended to picture her as a pink-colored pupa with no teeth. Being an only child, Ruth never had much contact with babies. Her mother assured her that a shortage of maternal instinct was hereditary on her side of the family.

Then Mary asked, "Are you still writing?" People always asked Ruth this even though, as far as she was concerned, there had never been any possibility of her stopping.

Ruth gave her stock answer. "I have to keep writing, I don't know how to do anything else." Which was probably true and usually good for a laugh at dinner parties.

When Ruth went back to bed, Steve was asleep. He left for Edmonton first thing Sunday morning. His band was playing at the Macdonald Hotel for two weeks. In the familiar confusion of his packing and promising and kissing goodbye, Ruth never did get around to telling him about Mary.

She'd been with Steve for four months now and for over half that time he'd been out on the road with the band. In her mind, Mary's visit was already shaping itself into one more anecdote she could rehearse, file away, and then retrieve to entertain Steve with when he got back. He always stayed at her place when he was in town.

The next Wednesday, just around suppertime, Ruth started cleaning the apartment. She assumed this was still a prerequisite to having company from out of province. Mary was to arrive at eight. Defensive in advance, Ruth decided against changing her jeans and brushed her teeth instead.

The bus, for once, was on time.

At the front door, Mary hugged Ruth hard into her shiny sweet-smelling hair. They kissed each other, laughing. Ruth realized this was something they'd never done before, not even once in fifteen years.

Mary took Ruth by both hands and held her at arms' length, saying, "Just let me look at you."

Mary was beautiful and Ruth understood that this was not at all what she'd been expecting. She'd probably been feeling sorry for Mary for years. She noticed first, and then felt guilty for noticing first, that Mary's skin had finally cleared up, even the pock marks were gone. Her thin blonde hair was still long but now curled softly around her face like leaves. And she had contact lenses, blue ones. Her dress was blue too, running down into a complicated print of turquoise and yellow parrots at the hem.

Mary could have been, Ruth thought, one of those women she invariably saw on the Eighth Avenue Mall in Calgary, one of those women who was always wearing red lipstick, a pastel linen suit, high-heeled sandals with no pantyhose, and who was always just on her way into or out of some tall glass building, amiably ignoring the nice young man in the three-piece suit who was always holding the door for her. She could have been one of those women who always made Ruth want to get contact lenses and a perm.

Mary said, "You haven't changed a bit."

That's what Ruth was afraid of.

In the kitchen, Ruth offered coffee first but Mary said she'd prefer a drink. Ruth stood on a chair and got the bottle of rye down from the cupboard over the fridge. Mary settled herself at the kitchen table, crossing her legs and arranging her skirt. She took a pack of cigarettes and a slim gold lighter out of her purse. Her hands, creamed, manicured and remarkably still, were perfect.

When they were younger, Ruth recalled, they'd never questioned the fact that they would one day pass magically from gritty adolescence to lustrous womanhood. The change, they were certain, would be sudden and magnificent. With its arrival, they knew they would at long last be released from all fear and unhappiness and so would enter together into a life-long state of serenity and self-satisfaction. They would never again be sick, lonely, mad or silly, and could not be punished by anyone for anything. They seemed always to have known that innocence was a dangerous and ridiculous condition to find yourself in for any length of time.

While they were waiting to be transformed, they discussed the way they would style their hair, the clothes they would buy, the meals they would cook, and the parties they would give for each other's birthdays. They studied sex in a library book and were disturbed to learn that newlyweds are likely to have sex every night, but agreed that by then they would be able to endure anything.

Now Mary was sipping her drink and complaining pleasantly enough about the long boring train ride and the plans for the wedding. There were five other bridesmaids and Mary couldn't understand why anyone should have to subject themselves to bright blue velvet in this heat. And who did Debbie, the bride, think she was fooling with that expensive white dress?

Whenever Ruth thought of weddings, there seemed to be something smoky about them. This had to do with diamond rings compared in the girls' washroom during the last year of high school. Right after Christmas vacation, the new diamond rings returned to classes in a herd. Girls who'd hated each other since Grade Nine became bosom buddies on the strength of getting engaged on the same day, either Christmas morning or New Year's Eve. They would assemble in the washroom between classes, sit around on the floor and discuss wedding dresses while smoking hot butts with stiff left hands. The butts sizzled out and unrolled in the toilets when the bell rang.

In Aurora, it seemed, weddings had fallen into disuse. Ruth had only been to one in the five years she'd lived there. It was an informal gathering at the couple's apartment but even then, the guests all seemed slightly embarrassed until the groom brought out some beer and turned up the stereo. The whole idea of marriage was something Ruth sneered at, they all did, and yet there they were, toasting and kissing and congratulating the happy couple who'd been living together in that apartment for years. Ruth couldn't imagine the feeling of wanting to marry someone who was also wanting to marry you back. Afterwards she was depressed for days, failing to find the expected satisfaction in thinking that no one had ever, at least not to her knowledge, felt that way about her.

While Ruth mixed two more drinks, Mary admired the apartment which was compact and crowded with secondhand furniture, big colored pillows, photographs and posters, and hundreds of books. Ruth often thought that one of the finest pleasures of living alone was being able to watch all your belongings spread out around you and no one else could complain or rearrange them. Mary said, "It's just like you, Ruth, just the way I imagined it would be."

Ruth thought Mary had it all now, that combination of power, self-control and stylishness they'd been so impatient and so prepared for when they were younger. She couldn't imagine Mary being afraid of anything anymore.

Ruth, on the other hand, was still waiting to feel like a grown-up. She was still prone to eating pepperoni pizza while having slobbering hysterics at four in the morning. She had yet to get anything besides sore knees out of washing her kitchen floor and she'd never seriously considered waxing it. Babies still intimidated her, laundry depressed her, clothing stores made her cranky, and she bubbled with resentment when she ran out of soap in the shower and found that her mother wasn't standing right outside the bathroom door with another bar. Sometimes she still wished she could go back to the time when she was living with her parents and going to university, gorging herself on literature and logic and her mother's rare roast beef. Her parents were proud of her and she'd been safe then, not yet needing to be strong or cynical or organized.

Mary took a picture out of her green leather bag. It was Lee-Ann on her third birthday, smiling out of the lace collar of a frothy white dress with little red hearts on it. She was born on Valentine's Day. Her hair, blonde and straight like Mary's, was tied up in pigtails with two red ribbons. Ruth thought she looked happy, pretty, and very bright. Mary said she was looking for a baby brother. "Maybe next year."

Lee-Ann was with her grandmother while Mary was away. Ruth wondered why David couldn't look after her. Mary said, "He has a hard enough time babysitting the nights I have my yoga, never mind for two weeks straight," as though it were obvious and rather lovable, to married women and mothers at least, that there are some things you just can't expect of men because they just aren't capable of doing them. Ruth nodded as though she too understood and approved of this principle. "Besides," Mary said, "Mom just loves having her, the only grandchild so far, you know."

Mary had four brothers. Ruth had always thought this should mean she was spoiled, but instead she was ignored. Mr. and Mrs. Yurick seemed to assume that, being a girl, the worst problems Mary would ever have were acne and myopia. Mrs. Yurick, Ruth thought even then, never expected much of anything, good or bad, from Mary. It was the boys who needed to be looked after, protected from drugs, alcohol, wild girls, and fast cars. They were all still in Hastings, the four of them saved now and sensibly acquiring steady jobs, nice wives and brand-new houses.

From what Mary said, it appeared that Mrs. Yurick found her more interesting, more likeable even, now that she was married and a mother herself.

"How's your mother?" Mary asked.

Ruth still envied those chummy mother-daughter duos she would see having afternoon coffee in the Aurora Café, chatting and gossiping, exchanging advice and complaints about husbands, helping each other on with their fur-collared coats, just like they were old friends. Ruth was sure that she and her own mother would never manage that. Ruth figured her mother would never consider her an adult person until she either published a book or got married, preferably the latter.

For years Ruth's mother always told her, "Just live together, don't bother getting married, it's not worth it." She also said she had no great burning desire to be a grandmother anyway.

But lately, as Ruth passed twenty-five and kept on going, her mother had started asking pointed questions. She kept bringing up the married cousins back in Hastings who were all expecting a second child by now but were still decorating their new houses all by themselves, and the unmarried cousins, also back in Hastings, who were all getting diamond rings for Christmas and registering their china and crystal at McCartney's. She had some trouble keeping the names in Ruth's letters straight and was always asking about some man Ruth hadn't seen for two months.

Ruth's father, who seldom expressed an opinion on anything not political or automotive, declared that he would still love her anyway, no matter what she did, and to hell with what her mother said.

After the picture of Lee-Ann, Ruth felt they weren't talking enough and she thought it was her fault since they were, after all, in her apartment. So she came up with a picture for Mary, an old one which, for reasons she had never contemplated, she still carried in her wallet.

In the picture, they are standing, five girls, in front of the Hastings Airport, squinting into the sun. The humid August heat is somehow palpable, emanating perhaps from the burnt-looking sidewalk or the swollen grey shadows behind them. Mary recognized it immediately as the day she and the other three left for school in Toronto. Ruth was the only one staying behind in Hastings where she would begin university three weeks later.

Mary handed back the picture, shook her head and said fondly, "You're so different, Ruth, you were always so different."

In the picture, Mary and the other girls, Doris, Shelley, and Sandra, are all wearing their summer dress pants, white or pale blue or beige, with matching short-sleeved flowered blouses on top. Sandra has a white cardigan folded over one arm. Doris and Shelley are standing arm in arm. Mary, on the right, is holding one hand to her forehead, shielding her eyes from the sun. Ruth is on the far left, wearing the baggy blue jeans her mother hates and the purple Indian cotton shirt she bought that summer at the fair. All down the front of her shirt there are embroidered flowers and little round mirrors which are flashing in the sunlight.

Ruth supposed that Mary was right — she had been different, still liked to think of herself that way. But sometimes now she suspected a change in tone, some modification in herself that she couldn't quite get at. On bad days, she wondered if being different might have stopped being her natural condition and become instead a set of precious irregularities which she practised and used as a talisman against the rest of the world, flashing it into people's eyes to disarm and then charm them, like the mirrors on her purple shirt.

Ruth thought Mary was distressingly conventional, something which she never allowed herself to be. Occasionally though, she would surprise herself in the act. Like that day in the laundromat when the hum of the machines lulled her into a picturesque fantasy of herself folding some nice man's shorts with the baby propped up, gurgling, against the orange laundry basket. She stopped herself but not in time to keep some kind of energy, some secret hope, from washing down through her arms and legs and then out, a greasy smear all over the linoleum. It was the same feeling she got when she thought of all those young couples sitting inside their new cedar houses on a cold snowy evening, and she could not imagine what on earth they might be doing, and she suspected that no one would ever tell her and she would never know how to do whatever it was two people did together to pass the time.

They were just getting ready for bed when Mary, who would spend the night on the couch, discovered the old high school yearbooks on the bottom bookshelf. She flipped through the pages of pictures and called out familiar names to Ruth who was in the bathroom washing her face. "Marjorie Hicks, do you remember Marjie? Lionel MacKay, didn't he die or something? And Jeanette Labelle, you wouldn't know her to see her!"

Ruth made a pot of tea and they looked through the yearbooks for a long time, sitting on the floor with the books spread open between them, Ruth in her flannelette nightgown, Mary in the green bathrobe. They hooted at their former selves and groaned at their former heart-throbs and tried to outdo each other with silly memories and imaginary fates for the people they'd never liked. They laughed so hard they had to pound the floor and hold onto their stomachs or sometimes each other. Ruth realized she hadn't considered the possibility of having fun with Mary.

Pointing to one picture, Mary asked, "Do you ever hear from Allan?"

"No, I don't."

Mary said he'd married someone else a year after Ruth left Hastings, some woman she didn't know but who was reportedly cruel and beautiful. Allan was working at the Hastings City Hall now, something to do with building permits, issuing or inspecting them. Mary said, "I never understood how you could spend three whole years with Allan and then not marry him. Didn't you feel like you'd wasted your time?"

Ruth couldn't begin to explain it all now. She'd just never looked at Allan as someone to marry. But after five years of relative silence, broken only by Christmas cards and the occasional newsy note, she didn't know how to retrace for Mary the complications, the reasons, the decisions that should have been difficult but weren't. After five years, they had only the facts to go on.

The first three years had been chronicled in fat late-night letters and the odd phone call, while Ruth went to university in Hastings and Mary quit school and sampled a variety of low-paying jobs all over Toronto. Ruth graduated and moved to Alberta about the same time Mary brought David home to Hastings and married him. Soon they were both too busy for letters. Ruth had a good government job in Aurora and a singular, unhealthy relationship with a man named Jim White. Mary had Lee-Ann, took the real estate course and went back to work. Ruth left Whitey after three years, quit her job to write full-time and began a long series of short but educational romances.

"Where's Bart these days?" Mary asked abruptly. Bart was

one of Ruth's old lovers. She'd been with him at Christmas and, feeling optimistic at the time, had mentioned him in all her Christmas cards. Between Bart and Steve there'd also been Don but Ruth skimmed over him because he'd only lasted a week and she was anxious to get to the good part, the past four months with Steve. She could just imagine how it all looked to Mary — the same way it looked to her mother no doubt — a parade of penises with no prospects.

She told Mary all about Steve, every romantic detail she could think of — the songs he'd written for her, the impulsive weekend at Calgary's best hotel, the roses for her birthday, the way he jumped up every night and did the dishes so Ruth could just relax and read the paper. She wanted Mary to know she was all right now. She wanted Mary to envy her.

"I have the best of both worlds," Ruth said. "All the advantages of living alone when Steve's away, and all the advantages of living together when he's in town. All the advantages with none of the disadvantages. This arrangement suits me fine."

She'd used it before, this vision of secure independence, used the same words to draw women to her, to dazzle them and then make them see how discontented they really were. Mary quarrelled with the word "arrangement" which she said sounded mercenary.

Ruth showed her a picture of Steve. Mary admired his brown eyes which looked deep and warm in the picture. But Ruth was angry because he hadn't called for over a week so she said they didn't look that good in real life. But then she felt guilty and kept working his name into the conversation so Mary would know they were serious about each other.

Just after they'd gone to bed, Mary called out in the dark, "Did I tell you Andrea says hello? She's fine, just fine. We talk on the phone every day."

In high school Andrea Gray had been the other, less-committed member of their trio, serving mainly as a handy alternate best friend whenever Ruth and Mary weren't speaking to each other.

When they were all seventeen, Andrea tried to kill herself with aspirins. Ruth had since wondered why they weren't surprised and why they just assumed she'd done it for no particular reason. Ruth and Mary went to visit her in the psychiatric ward and afterwards Mary said, "How could she let us down like this?"

Two months later Andrea met and married Earl Burnett. They rented a house in the country. They had to go on welfare and whenever Earl got angry, he would throw his supper at Andrea's head. She got pregnant and the baby, a boy, was born dead. Ruth and Mary went to visit her in the hospital and were outraged to think they'd kept her in the maternity ward with all the happy mothers and their pretty babies.

Then Andrea had an affair with Earl's best friend, John Jackowski, who rented their spare room. Everybody knew about it except Earl who left her when he found out. Andrea married John, who came from a wealthy family, and they built a ranch-style house on ten acres of land. Andrea got pregnant and had a nine-pound baby boy. Earl went to visit her in the hospital and apologized for everything so Andrea named the baby after him. John became a teacher. Andrea got pregnant and had a girl this time and then she got her tubes tied but almost died from an infection. Earl married a girl named Louise so Andrea, John and the kids all went to the wedding. By then, Andrea was twenty-two, Mary was back in Hastings with David Barnes, and Ruth had just moved to Aurora.

But now Andrea was fine, Mary said she was fine.

Ruth lay awake in the dark for a long time, wondering how Andrea could ever be fine, how she could possibly have come through all that and still end up just like everyone else. Ruth imagined that her skin must still be the same even now, the humid color of sliced mushrooms, vanilla-scented. What was the point then of going through and surviving such pain if it did not leave a mark on you?

The next morning Ruth got up late after lying there for nearly an hour, mostly awake but sometimes dozing in and out. She listened to Mary in the kitchen, opening all the cupboards in search of the coffee, boiling some water, opening the fridge for the milk, turning the pages of a magazine. It was comforting.

When Ruth came out of the bedroom, Mary was sitting at the kitchen table in her bathrobe, reading a magazine Ruth had shown her the night before, the one with her new article in it.

"Good morning."

"Morn." Ruth had always been inarticulate in the morning.

Mary kept reading and then said, "You're so lucky, Ruth," with a broad gentle gesture that took in everything — the bright yellow cupboards, the blue countertop, the magazine, the floor-to-ceiling bookshelves in the living room, the oak desk, the filing cabinet, all the other books piled on every flat surface, and Ruth in her nightgown too.

Ruth didn't know Mary well enough anymore to tell whether she meant it or not. She didn't think so though. Afterwards Ruth would wonder why she found it easier to believe that Mary pitied, rather than admired, her.

She couldn't make out Mary's mood but she gave her stock reply anyway, trying to make her laugh. "It wasn't luck at all, just good birth control." Ruth thought she wanted to hear what was on Mary's mind so she added, "You're not doing too badly yourself, are you?"

Mary brightened up and started talking about Lee-Ann and the good day care center she'd just discovered.

Then she started talking vaguely about a girl named Lisa whom, Ruth remembered, she'd mentioned several times the night before. Ruth had assumed she was someone Mary worked with but now it seemed that Lisa was David's friend, not Mary's, a fellow student in the Psychology course. Lisa, as it turned out, was in love with David and they were having an affair. Mary did not suggest a reason for the affair, but seemed to take it for granted, speaking of it in the same way she spoke of marriage, as a foregone conclusion.

Mary knew all about it because David told her everything just the way he always had. Mary said, "He knows I understand him. If he wouldn't talk to me about it, then I'd be worried." She was very calm and Ruth didn't have to say anything.

Mary knew all about Lisa, she'd even met her once at a student party although she wasn't sure if they were already having the affair then or not. Mary said Lisa had long black hair and lived in a single room not far from the university. She rode a motorcycle in the summer so David bought her a new bell helmet for her twentieth birthday which was in March. Every Thursday Lisa and David went for pizza after their night class and then they went back to her room. He never spent the whole night with her though. Mary said, "Poor kid, she thinks he'll leave me for her. But I'm not worried, things like that don't happen anymore. I know he doesn't love her, he can't live without me."

She was talking quickly now, with her head down, eyes focusing on the edge of the table, her feet, on the floor. Her elegant hands, fluttering up to her throat and then flopping back, palms up, into her lap, were like pigeons.

With a ballooning sense of horror, Ruth imagined the two of them, Mary and David, sitting at the dining room table after supper, having their coffee or maybe a cosy liqueur, discussing "the problem." Lee-Ann, in pigtails and miniature denim overalls, was shovelling an artichoke from one side of her plate to the other. Mary and David were making fun of little Lisa; David might mimic her walk or her silly snorting laugh. Mary would laugh then too and pat his hand across the thousand-dollar oval teak table. They would sabotage the girl's thin hopes with their generous conjugal maturity. Ruth didn't feel sorry for Mary because Mary was making sure it was clear there was no reason to.

Ruth went into the bedroom to get dressed. Mary followed her, still talking, coffee cup in hand, and sat down on the unmade bed. She admired the sheets, which were brown with orange flowers and green leaves.

Ruth rummaged around in the dresser for a clean teeshirt. She felt uneasy undressing in front of another woman. It reminded her of being in the girls' locker room after Grade Nine gym class and they were all wearing baggy blue gym suits with their first names embroidered across the back and Ruth was silently suffering her lack of noticeable breasts and the smell of her own sweat, while the other girls, and Mary too, bounded around the steamy room, snapping each other's bra straps and admiring themselves. She thought now of turning her back to Mary but decided it would be childish.

Mary was saying, "Do you remember how we always agreed that if our husbands were ever unfaithful, even just once, we would leave them and go live together in a nice apartment with our kids and some cats?"

Ruth remembered how often this prospect had sounded more appealing to her than what they would have to do if their husbands were true-blue.

Mary said cheerfully, "It was a relief to find out that's not what you have to do after all. It really hasn't made that much difference to me, I know it's only a physical thing." Ruth wondered why married women liked to dismiss sexual attraction as trivia, forgetting how it could make everything in the world that you'd ever took pleasure in, books, music, mountains, lobster, seem pale and foolish, merely a series of distractions to help pass the time until you could lie down beside him again.

"I'm not afraid of Lisa," Mary said. "I'm not afraid of

87

anything anymore . . . . It's David who's afraid now, he's afraid she might kill herself if he stops seeing her. I try to reassure him though, I tell him it's not likely that anybody would love him that much. I tell him real life isn't like that."

Just around noon, Ruth walked Mary to the bus stop which was actually the drugstore on Main Street. The upper storey of the building was being renovated and raw planks stuck out through the window-holes like severed limbs. Someone dropped a hammer from the upper scaffold; there was much imaginative cursing from down below but no injuries.

All the businesses in Aurora were assembled on three blocks of Main Street, which was crowded now with cars, dogs, and people all busy with the intricacies of summer. Ruth imagined people all over town tanning, bicycling, sweating, buying briquets, and wishing for convertibles and cold beer. Their children by now were probably pickled in pink lemonade.

The heat was already building. There would be a thunderstorm when the sun went down. The mountains ringing the river valley in which Aurora sat were hazy and blue, flat with no shadows, no shape.

"It's like a cradle," Mary said enthusiastically. Which was true enough, but not something anyone who lived there would ever have said out loud.

A group of people stood in a knot outside the post office, gesturing at each other with postcards and phone bills, paying no attention to the mountains. They all, Ruth knew, kept their private counsel with the mountains, took from them what they needed, did not presume to discuss them beyond admiring them when they went pink with the sunrise in summer or avalanched and killed tourists in the winter. The mountains, they knew, were not merely surfaces, were rock all the way through. Parts of them, stratified intestines, had nothing to do with seeing at all.

The bus to Calgary was late so Ruth suggested they wait in the Aurora Café across the street. On the sidewalk in front, a German Shepherd lay stretched out on its side, sleeping or dead. Two women with baby strollers and bags full of groceries sidestepped the dog without looking down.

Inside, the café booths (obligatory orange vinyl patched with black electrical tape) were all filled with workmen on their lunch hour, wearing hard hats, dusty denim shirts, and yellow steel-toed boots. Ruth and Mary found two stools at the counter. Doreen, the waitress, cook, and dishwasher, stood behind the counter filling salt shakers and humming a modified version of "Onward Christian Soldiers." Her white uniform was splattered in odd places with mustard and ketchup.

Mary was once again wearing her blue sun-dress and two or three of the workmen stared at her, not being rude, just curious. Ruth knew some of them and smiled. Tomorrow they would ask her, teasing, "Where's your friend?"

Over coffee and grilled cheese sandwiches, Mary asked Ruth, "Do you think you'll get married?"

Ruth misunderstood, thinking it first a rhetorical, then an irrelevant, and finally a nosy question.

She thought of her cousin Denise back in Hastings whom she had always been told had married late in life. For years, the whole family had treated Denise with a hopeful sympathy, as though there were little else she could be expected to do at such an advanced age besides marry a widower or keep working forever at the Bank of Montreal. Ruth had recently figured out that Denise actually got married at twenty-eight. Her husband, Howard Machuk, was a gynecologist who'd never been married and he gave her everything she could possibly want, including a dishwasher for her thirty-first birthday. So the family had finally relaxed, except for the fact that Denise kept working when she didn't have to anymore, and they would never have family now because it was too late.

Mary simplified the question. "You and Steve, I mean." She picked through her sandwich and pulled out two dill pickle slices.

Steve Schroeder, who was thirteen years older than Ruth although he didn't look it, had been married twice already and had two complete families living in British Columbia, a son and a daughter in each, both with new fathers now. Ruth had never looked at Steve as someone to marry. Mary said she could see her point.

"Oh, don't worry," Mary said. "You'll get married some day, everyone does. It's so nice to get all that high romance stuff over and done with, to have everything settled for once and for all, to know you don't have to be alone ever again."

After all that Mary had told her, Ruth wished she was joking, but she wasn't.

The bus arrived and Mary got on, calling back promises to say hello to everybody back in Hastings for Ruth.

The next night was Friday so Ruth walked over to the bar. She put on a skirt, pale green with pink wild roses, and a white halter top because it was too hot. Being the only bar in town, the Aurora Hotel, decorated with barn wood and antique sepia photographs, was where everyone went to meet everyone else on Friday night.

Ruth sat with some friends and drank beer and then Scotch, which was her favorite. Mostly she talked to a man named Martin MacDougall whom she'd met at a barbecue the weekend before. He was an ex-high school teacher from Prince Edward Island who was now a divorced carpenter living in Aurora. Picking up where he'd left off at the barbecue, he told Ruth the rest of his life story and bought her a couple of drinks.

When Martin got up to leave just after midnight, Ruth went with him. They walked to his house which was just two blocks from hers. He took off his shirt in the kitchen and got out more beer. He wasn't talking, and he didn't seem to notice or, if he did notice, he didn't find it strange that Ruth was silently crying.

When they went into the bedroom there were no curtains on the window and no sheets on the bed. He said he'd just done the laundry.

After a few minutes, Ruth sat up and retied her halter top. At first Martin wouldn't let go of her hand and then he got angry and started swearing and shaking his fist at her. At first she felt sorry for him but then she laughed to herself at how foolish he looked lying there on the bare mattress with his pants down around his ankles and his skin showing white in the darkness. Her own bare feet looked like wax on the tile.

She didn't give much thought to Steve who hadn't called her for two weeks anyway. It was something of a relief to discover that she didn't care whether either one of them liked her or not. She'd often wondered why women spend so much time doing things to make men fall or stay in love with them, while the men all expect to be loved just the way they are. There was a certain freedom in not wanting to fall or be in love. Ruth figured she could probably do just about anything now.

Putting on her sandals in Martin's back porch, she thought maybe she hadn't really gone there planning to have sex anyway. But she quickly gave up trying to convince herself. There was, she supposed, some tacit agreement between two people who left the bar together after midnight on Friday night. She knew this was true in Aurora anyway. She didn't know what rules other people in other places might have made for themselves.

There were no lights on Martin's street. The night sky was so densely black that Ruth would never have guessed there were mountains inside it if she hadn't known better. She started walking home, then turned back and cut across Martin's yard to the next street which was the long way home but well-lit. She was glad to think there was no one at home that she would have to tell the whole story to, complete with insightful suggestions as to what this might or might not have to do with Mary, and humorous remarks about still being afraid of the dark at her age.

HISTORIES

ANNE AND PETER DICKSON used to live in southern Ontario. Then they went west to Alberta, just like a lot of other people. They settled in Lairdmore, a small town in the Rockies. Peter said Lairdmore was a boom town where there would always be work and they would always be happy.

Peter, who was a carpenter, built them a house in the new subdivision at the south end of town. In this part of Lairdmore, all the streets were named after indigenous birds and animals: Porcupine Place, Fox Avenue, Sparrow Street, Marmot Boulevard.

Anne and Peter lived on Cougar Crescent where all the houses were new. The street usually smelled of fresh paint and of wood burning in all the new stone fireplaces. Most of the houses were either white aluminum siding or white stucco and had a sled, a stroller or a German Shepherd parked in the front yard. In the winter, each yard was bisected by a precisely shovelled sidewalk. Often there were small children playing on the snowbanks and the snow would fall back onto the sidewalk in chunks. The families in these houses were all young and they all knew each other. They compared their mortgage payments, their children's report cards, and their grocery bills. One or another of the wives was always having a dinner party, an affair, or a minor operation. They all appeared to be more or less content.

Soon after they moved in, Anne sent a photograph of herself and Peter standing in front of their new house back to her family in Ontario. Her mother mailed back a batch of recipes and wrote, *Annie, you're so thin, so thin I wouldn't know you. The house is nice though.* Nobody else except Peter called her Annie anymore — Annie was obviously somebody else, a much fatter person.

In Ontario, Anne had worked for a small commercial photography studio, Eberhardt and Associates. They shot weddings, postcards, family portraits and baby pictures. When she and Peter moved to Lairdmore, Anne decided it was time to try a different approach. Peter teased her about wanting to be an artist. (All the aspiring artists they'd known in Ontario were convinced they could become "real" artists if only they were given half a chance. "Half a chance" usually meant being spared the need to earn a living, cook hamburgers, and clean the toilet.) But Anne knew that Peter was proud of her.

She carried her camera with her everywhere. She thought there would never be an end to the number of things in Lairdmore that should be photographed. She took up cross-country skiing because she saw it as a way to get closer to what she wanted to see. She could not have explained precisely what it was that she was after, but she assumed that it, like most things of value, would never be found by ordinary or easy means.

At first Anne limited her skiing to several afternoons a week on the Lairdmore Golf Course. After two weeks she felt competent enough to attempt something more challenging. One morning just after Peter had left for work, Anne packed herself a lunch and put on her new down parka, her grey wool knickers, and a pair of thick red socks. With her black hair spurting out from under a tight yellow toque, her head looked like a fat sunflower.

Carrying her skis, poles, and a small backpack which held ski wax, her lunch, her camera and extra film, Anne left the house and headed for the far edge of town. The morning cold was solid and extreme, like a capsule forming itself around her body.

The snow crunched under her boots like broken shells and her scarf swooped out behind her in the wind.

It was still early and the streets were quiet. In most of the houses Anne passed, only one or two rooms somewhere near the back were lit, kitchens in the morning, warm yellow squares. All the furnaces were on, waving flags of white smoke. Frosted-up cars, still plugged in, were warming up in the driveways, disappearing inside their own exhaust clouds.

Walking backwards against the wind, Anne watched thin clouds unraveling around the mountains, shredding on the high peaks. The snow and the immaculate morning light brought out every formation of the rock, outlining each crack and knob in precise detail.

Lairdmore sat in an oval-shaped river valley, tightly ringed by mountains on all sides. Sometimes, when Anne could no longer imagine a road actually coiling its way through all that rock, she thought of the valley as an island with no way to get off. This was not an unpleasant feeling.

In about fifteen minutes, Anne had reached the far edge of town. Close to the coal mine that had brought Lairdmore into being a hundred years before, there were no sidewalks and no street names here. The houses, which were owned by the mine and leased to the miners, were all made of wood, improvised, unstructured — jazz music. The yards were full of assorted accumulations — gutted cars, old tires, a bathtub still up on legs and filled with tin cans and rusty gears. Anne thought she could smell something like kerosene and bread mould mixed together but then decided she was only imagining it.

She walked past one house with two green wooden lawn chairs still sitting out in front, mounded with snow and frozen to the ground. She stopped to pet a round black cat that came rubbing around her ankles, purring, its whiskers stiff and white with frost. It looked like a walrus.

The miners' houses were black with coal dust, another

accumulation, one they would never be able to get rid of now. The windward sides of the trees were black too and the miners' children might grow up believing that trees everywhere were supposed to be black on one side. The mine itself was out of sight, around the corner beyond a dense group of evergreens. A square blue engine pulling twenty coal cars behind it was switching from the main track onto the spur, squealing on the cold rails.

Just beyond the last house, Anne stopped to wait for a ride up the gravel road to Bridgetown.

Peter disapproved of her hitch-hiking. "You never know what you're letting yourself in for, Annie," he'd warned several times. "I really wish you wouldn't. It's not safe, or smart either. There's a lot of sick people in this world." Peter expected nothing but the worst from strangers.

He also disapproved of her skiing alone. When she'd told him several days before of her plan to ski up to Bridgetown, he said, "What if you fall and break a leg? Or you could get lost, you know. I'd never find you. And there are wild animals up there too, you know, bears. I'd worry about you, Annie, out there all alone." Peter expected nothing but the worst from solitude.

He would disapprove of this day altogether.

He didn't disapprove of *everything* she did — only, he said, of those things that caused him to worry. (Peter seemed to think that all this busy worrying was something you just naturally took on when you got married.) The things that caused him to worry were numerous. His fear for her was sequential and cumulative. He stock-piled new dangers and flashed them out at her triumphantly. It became remarkably dangerous to go to the laundromat alone at night, to leave the house unlocked when she went out to the post office, to be friendly to strangers and stray dogs.

In Ontario, Anne had been afraid of everything too. The fear had been a gauzy vague discomfort and the bad dreams were persistent. In them she was always hiding, running, crying, or dying in unnatural and imaginative ways. The dreams had not recurred in Lairdmore. They might just as well have belonged to somebody else.

Anne turned her back to the wind and pressed one mitten to her left cheek where a patch of skin the size of a quarter was growing numb with the cold. Two or three cars passed by without stopping. Finally a lop-sided pickup truck pulled over and stopped. The truck was mottled black and primer red, burning oil in a dense blue cloud behind.

The driver pushed open the passenger door as Anne ran towards the truck, her ski poles banging against her shins. "Where you heading, miss?"

"Up to the Bridgetown Road," Anne said, leaning into the warmth of the cab and juggling her skis.

"Well, hop in then," the old man said amiably. "I'm going up that way myself. Just throw your gear in back."

Anne slid her skis and poles up over the tailgate which was green and tied shut with a twist of rusted baling wire.

She got into the cab, slapping her black leather mitts together like a seal. "Cold," she said, ducking her chin down inside the collar of her jacket.

"Cold, damn cold," the old man agreed vigorously. He was packed in tight behind the steering wheel in an army green parka. His breath had condensed in beads on the bright orange scarf that was wound several times around his neck. It might have been holding his head on. "I'm Herb Murchie," he said.

"Pleased to meet you, Mr. Murchie. I'm Anne Dickson."

"Oh, just call me Herb. Mr. Murchie's my pa and he's been dead twenty years now. I'm just Herb." He let go of the steering wheel to shake her hand. Wrapped in a double wool mitten, his hand felt like a pile of old socks. "You must be new in town."

"I've been here for over a year now," Anne said. But she knew that to the old-timers even families who'd lived in Lairdmore for ten years or more were still "the new folks up the road aways." And the old-timers were all tangibly proud of the position they held in Lairdmore, which was quickly becoming a community of newcomers, most of them wandering in from Ontario and other parts east.

"Myself, I been here for seventy years," Herb said. "When I was a kid, weren't more than twenty houses here altogether. Just that, the mine and the company store. My pa was mine foreman and my cousin Jake, he ran the store. Stole licorice from old Jake. Never amounted to much of a thief though, I was always getting caught with black teeth and a stash in my sock drawer." He laughed and offered Anne a sticky peppermint from a bag on the dash. "Still got a sweet tooth though."

Herb smiled shinily with perfect teeth and gums of an unlikely peach color. He sucked hard on two peppermints at once, clicking them against his teeth.

They were silent as the road lifted them up out of the valley and crossed a fresh avalanche chute. The passageway that had been chopped through the snow was just wide enough to admit one vehicle. The compacted snow on either side stood in solid six-foot banks mottled with boulders and branches.

"Nice trip, the ski up to Bridgetown," Herb said. "Still do it myself, the odd time. Mostly though I just like to drive up and take a look around, like I'm doing today. But the place is nothing now. When I was a kid, must have been five hundred people lived up there."

Bridgetown, like Lairdmore, had been a coal town. The mine had chopped streets out of the mountain like steps and put up over a hundred houses for the workers and their families. The Bridgetown women put in big vegetable gardens behind the houses and chickens ran loose in the yards. All the men worked for the mine.

Since coming to Lairdmore, Anne had read several histories of the area. Many of them were actual journals kept by explorers and settlers who'd first come to the mountains. She also bought a book on mountain flowers, a field guide to rocks and minerals, and a full-color catalogue of mountain wildlife. The books settled themselves around the house . . . Flowers in the kitchen, Wildlife in the bathroom, Explorers on the top of the digital clock-radio on the bedside table. She propped Flowers up against the kettle and studied the identification key while she washed the supper dishes.

When Peter first noticed the new books straying all over the house, he said, "What do you need all these books for anyway?" Peter assumed there must be a reason for everything.

"I like them," Anne said.

"Is that the only reason?"

"Well . . . I suppose they're educational."

Peter said, unconvinced, "I suppose." He believed that Anne never did anything for the obvious reasons. Once he'd told her he was proud of the fact that she wasn't a simple woman. As if, Anne thought some time later, that meant nobody could expect him to understand her anyway.

The road narrowed to a single lane and disappeared in a tight curve to the right. Herb pounded the horn twice to warn any oncoming traffic. On the right, the road hugged a sandy embankment so steep that it was completely bare of snow. On the left, there was nothing but a small pull-off space in case of emergencies. The road was icy and even at ten miles an hour the back tires of the truck began to spin uselessly. Anne stared nervously over the edge, willing the truck around the corner, but Herb never stopped talking about Bridgetown. It was as though, Anne thought, he wanted to be sure she knew both where she was going and what she'd be missing when she got there.

He'd gone to school in Bridgetown. "We fed the elk right

out the window," he told her. "They'd eat right out of your hand, slobber all down your arm. Aunt Mary Margaret, she was the schoolteacher, brought apples for them. But she's dead now."

The whole mountain seemed to be riddled with his relatives. Most of them were likely long dead by now, but no less a part of the family for that.

Anne smiled and nodded but Herb needed little encouragement to go on. "In those days," he reminisced, "Bridgetown was quite the place. There was the smithy and Ike Bacon's drugstore where he sold liquor out of the icebox in back and the big general store with everything from long johns to playing cards and duck eggs. My cousin Gertie, she gave piano lessons in a room up over the drugstore. There was even a whorehouse, course I wasn't supposed to know about that. The two churches, Presbyterian and R.C., they were always fighting back and forth to see who'd have Friday night bingo. I won a turkey from the R.C.'s once but my ma, she wouldn't cook it seeing as how we were Presbyterian."

Anne imagined Bridgetown's terraced streets perpetually filled with bingo players and buggies and apple-chewing elk.

"Here's the turnoff now," Herb said, pumping the brakes and guiding the truck onto a road to the right. "I'll take you in to the first bridge. Can't go no further with the truck though, road's not plowed past that."

Anne pulled off her toque and shook out her hair which was damp and curling with sweat. Herb jiggled the knob on the heater but nothing happened. "Stuck wide open all year round," he explained, shaking his head and untying his scarf.

Anne was glad to stay and listen that much longer. Herb knew all the histories of the valley, remembered everything, piled up stories and years one on top of the other like layers of rock. But he didn't seem to think of the things he remembered as history, didn't appear to structure time the way other people did, in a straight line from past to present with three dots at the end for the future. There was something circular in the way he spoke of all those years. They were all of a piece, a single sphere enclosed by the continuity and the limits, birth and death, of his own life . . . a crystal globe looking in all directions at once. The space of time between then and now was curving in a great arc which would join back to itself in the end. Herb spoke as though he saw no reason why anything should have changed in the first place and no reason why it shouldn't all change back again one day.

Anne thought of her own family back in Ontario. None of them, not even the old aunts and the great-uncles, told stories like Herb did. Maybe they didn't have any, maybe they'd always been just the way they were now. Anne could only remember being told one story, the one about Uncle Amos being struck dead by lightning on the Hallsey Golf Course one Saturday afternoon. His nine-iron was welded into his hands. And that story was only told at weddings and funerals. The rest of her relatives had lived quietly without taking notes and then died quietly without making a fuss. In Anne's family, eccentricity was considered impolite.

Peter came from a large family too but his relatives turned out to be no more entertaining than her own. There was one woman, Aunt India, who'd suffered what the rest of the family called "a nervous experience" when she reached menopause. She'd sold her house in Lashing Heights and moved to Paris with an easel, a box of oil paints, and a Lhasa Apso pup named Chin. In the eyes of her family, the worst thing of all was the fact that she soon began to make a lot of money from her painting. If she'd failed, they could have loved her again and sent her the airfare home. The lives of all the other Dicksons were quite straightforward and Peter was just like them — his life persisted in falling neatly into place around him. Other people's life crises were simple decisions for Peter.

He'd passed through public school without undue trauma and through high school without undue study or stress. He'd gone on to university because it seemed appropriate at the time. He'd majored in Social Work because he liked people and thought he could help them simplify their lives. He'd dropped out in the middle of his third year because one day at lunch he realized he wouldn't be able to save the world anyway, with or without five years of education. He'd taken up carpentry because he was good with his hands and a man with a trade could always find work. He'd married for love. He was the most untortured person Anne had ever met.

Herb, who seemed to be following Anne's train of thought, said, "I even met my own true love in Bridgetown." Anne smiled encouragingly, wanting to hear more.

Herb went on. "Effie MacKay, her name was. My brother Leonard, we were mountain guides together then, he introduced us. Went to the dance every Saturday night just to see her. I took her a corsage every week for months just so she'd dance with me. Still wouldn't marry me though, corsage or no. She'd say, 'I'd rather be an old maid than a widow, Herb Murchie. You're going to kill yourself up there one of these days. I'm no fool,' she'd say. Then she'd flounce off and dance with somebody else. A hard woman, that Effie," Herb said, with fond admiration. "Course this was all before the bad times came."

The bad times for Bridgetown had begun with the 1928 explosion. Ten miners were killed and the town began to turn against the company. The men who survived refused to go back down inside the mine. They organized a strike for danger pay and better safety measures. After the Crash in 1929, the company could only afford to work the mine during the summer months. The people started packing up and moving down the mountain to Lairdmore where the higher quality coal meant year-round work. In a year and a half the Bridgetown Coal

Company was bankrupt. They burned down the tipple and sealed up the shaft. They tore down all the houses and Bridgetown was gone.

Anne was still wondering about Effie. "What happened to her when the town folded up?" she asked.

"She came down to Lairdmore too then and took a job teaching at the new school."

Anne imagined Effie, a stern young woman in a black bonnet, walking away from the town and down the mountain with a suitcase in one hand and a corsage in the other. There were men in black business suits tearing down her house behind her. The mountains were set in monochrome all around her, white snow, black trees like bristle brushes. Of course it was a cloudy day. Effie kept walking away, a hard woman with her suitcases (cardboard) full of tablecloths (linen) and silverware (sterling).

Herb continued. "Wasn't long before she up and married Ulysse Paquette."

"I'm sorry," Anne said. She'd been hoping for a happy ending.

"Oh don't be," Herb said, grinning. "She ended up a widow anyway. Ulysse, he died in a fire at the hotel he owned. Not the kind of thing you could lay odds on beforehand." Anne found it hard to smile along with Herb at Ulysse's misfortune.

"By then I was working in the Lairdmore mine, I was forty-five. Effie and me, we got married the next year. She wore a grey suit and an orchid. Never did figure out why she thought my being down inside the mountain was any safer than being up on top of it!" Anne was relieved to discover that it had all worked out in the end. There was some kind of basic reassurance to be derived from other people's happy endings. She felt like applauding but put on her toque and mittens instead. They were at the first bridge, where Herb would leave her. In the narrow road, he turned the truck around in little jerks until it was aimed back down the mountain towards Lairdmore. He got out and helped Anne lift her gear over the tailgate.

"Enjoy yourself," he called as he drove away. "Bridgetown'll always be the best place around these parts. You'll see."

Anne propped her ski poles up against an evergreen and positioned her feet on her skis, snapping the bindings shut with the tip of one pole. She could still hear Herb's truck grinding back out to the main road.

The bridge was made of logs, several of them rotted away now, forming dark crevasses in the snow. It was the first of three that had given Bridgetown its name. The creek below it flowed slick and garbled over the rocks, moving too quickly to freeze. Anne skied across carefully, her eyes tearing in the wind. She imagined the first explorers, the ones she'd been reading about, coming this same way . . . coming to this unnamed river in flood which must be crossed somehow if the pass was to be found and the country pushed through to the other side. They were all still here somehow.

You could only hear river sound rushing, a monstrous new pulse in your ears. The water came up to your neck, roped around your ankles. Food and clothing, three guns, swept away. Horses screaming. You might never be dry again.

Anne pulled her camera out of her pack and composed a shot of the bridge. She fitted her skis back into the fresh track and continued on. The track carried her forward, turning each corner in a smooth arc, leading her on like a map. If her skis slipped out of the track, they would sink deep into the new powder on either side.

You had nothing to go on, no trail, no map, no guarantee. Even the Indians didn't come this far, knew these mountains had nothing to offer but magic and myths. They were afraid. They had no names for the Shining Mountains. The rock was all one, no distance measured, no time either. No way to get through in miles or hours. The rock existing in a single dimension: space. You were pygmies.

The track went steadily uphill and Anne was beginning to sweat inside her parka. She loosened her scarf and unzipped her jacket a few inches to let in the cool air. She started to hum and then stopped, the little insect sound nervous and impossible in this place.

The trail took a sharp turn to the left. Slowing down abruptly, Anne lost the rhythm of her stride and struggled to stay in the track. Around the corner, the trees were thicker and more tangled, dead ones propped up against live ones, creaking under the weight of the snow, rotting away from the inside. The branches, which did not appear until several feet up each trunk, were growing blindly into each other. Anne photographed just the trunks, dismembered torsos, bodies without arms or legs, so many, so thin. But there was nothing horrible about them here. It was only carried away in the camera, spread out in the darkroom, hung in a frame on the wall, that they would become alarming or ridiculous.

You must have thought this an unfortunate land. Candelabra pine trees can only be beautiful once they no longer need to be journeyed through. They were the same trees, smaller then than now, but no less impossible. This place would not even be pleasant for another fifty years.

In some spots the trees were so thick that neither the sun nor the snow could get through to the ground. Here the grass sprouted like meagre hair through the frozen dirt.

Your crazy battered horses could never find enough grass to fill up their well-bred bellies. Ranging farther and farther, their hooves skidded on the wet rock. One dappled mare fell over the edge without crying out, still chewing.

The trail opened out of the trees, following the rim of an undercut cliff. Trying to plant her left pole, Anne jabbed first empty air and then a large chunk of snow and dirt that came loose and bounced down the cliff.

Her left knee, the closest to the dropoff, began to vibrate uncontrollably. Her thigh muscles clenched up tight and would not push forward. Her image of falling was large but not vivid, not extending much beyond the thought that Peter would disapprove if she died away up here when he didn't even know where she was.

The hardships were always borne. You never seemed to doubt that they could be, and you never seemed to be afraid of dying if they couldn't. Sewing-machine legs on the ledge sent pebbles like bullets over the edge. Your courage was genuine: you had no choice.

Anne pushed harder, leaning more on her poles, hauling herself up with the whole length of her arms. The trail rose more steeply, up over the second bridge and around a pile of boulders that had slid onto the old road. She'd imagined herself strong and severe on this mountain, taking the miles with ease and determined grace, but now her lungs were like bricks in her chest. She paused to wipe the sweat from the back of her neck and then leaned on her poles to rest, breathing deeply.

You thought of the old women back home serving high tea and teaching the little girls to embroider. Rock of Ages in cross-stitch. They had already stopped thinking about you. There was no way to reach you, too much rock in the way.

The trail dipped down to the third bridge. Anne brought her arms in close to her sides and pushed forward. She did not think about falling or stopping — either choice was more or less impossible.

A young woman — what was her name? — came with you, would not let her new husband go off alone this time. He was embarrassed and proud, you expected nothing but the worst . . . fainting, falling, complaints, she was bound to turn back after ten miles. But she tricked you all by being strong, silent, pregnant. The boy was born in a cave like an animal with no fur. Happy and howling, the two of them. You could do nothing but wait there three days while she healed (you were outraged by this indecent pain which you were supposed to be protected from) and nursed him and sang. It was hard to look at her because you knew she was braver than any of you.

Anne stopped on the last bridge, changed the lens on her camera, and focused far back into the trees.

This is a photograph of you, woman . . . see there, behind the big tree. No one will believe your stories. There is no way of knowing that you were ever here. The land closed up behind you like a mouth.

The trail took her into a large clearing. On the south side of the meadow, snow-covered terraces mounted the slope. Bridgetown had clung naturally to the mountain like a goat.

Still wearing her skis, Anne climbed awkwardly up to the third terrace and focused a long shot back down the slope.

This was a photograph of no one.

Still climbing, Anne watched the ground carefully, expecting artifacts, some archaeological sign just under the snow . . . a horseshoe maybe, or a broken dish with flowers painted in the bowl . . . discarded bits of lives like fingernails. But there was nothing. A promising lump in the snow turned out to be a dead squirrel.

On one of the upper streets she discovered one side of a concrete foundation still standing. It had been a large building, a church or maybe the school.

Even Herb Murchie's memories weren't real here. Effie wasn't here either, she was dead beneath the valley floor, her name and two dates like bookends carved in the granite. In the summer there might be red peonies on her grave.

There had been children born here. They were all in nursing homes now or dead, and the place on their birth certificates did not exist. They would always be children in Bridgetown, adults only in some other place. Anne tried to imagine families passing through high-ceilinged rooms on their way to dinner, school, the mine, cousin Gertie's piano school. She tried to imagine couples making love and could not put them into a big feather bed, but only onto the meadow, brushing away branches and pine cones before they laid down. Hard women, loved. Woman served up on the rock, bruises in a string down her backbone.

She climbed back down to the meadow and ate her lunch sitting on a bare rock in the sun.

It was almost dark by the time she got home.

She and Peter are eating supper at the blonde maple table which Peter built when they first moved in. The white dishes are like coins on the blue tablecloth. Two of Anne's photographs hang on the wall behind them but they aren't looking at them.

The first photograph is just above Peter's left shoulder. In it, an old man and an old woman are out in the backyard shelling peas. The white enamel bowl is wedged between their straight-backed wooden chairs.

Her dark dress is spotted with tiny colorless flowers like scars. His home-knit sweater is sagging brown and blue. Their faces lean together, rapt with green peas dropping into the bowl like beads from a broken bracelet.

They are stationed in front of a rock face which there is no reason for them to pay attention to.

The rock after rain is like some shiny metal.

The man and the woman cannot climb anymore . . . too old, too easily broken and bleeding . . . wingspan too short. They are pretending there is nothing behind them but sky. The woman's hand reaches down to ease the bandage around her tree-stump leg.

They look like crows but are not.

The second photograph is just above Peter's right shoulder. In it is an empty house which was torn down by the time Peter first saw the photograph. He couldn't remember where it had been.

White clapboard lists to the left, shedding overcooked shingles like flakes of sunburned skin.

There could have been a dinner table still there inside, set with white and silver for roast beef and carrots and lemon meringue. Anne doesn't expect Peter to be able to see inside because he still believes in the inherent solidity of walls.

There is no glass in the window frames which are peeling off in strips like cellophane tape. A blue curtain is flapping out through one of the holes. You can see right through the house. It has no intestines. You can see right through to the mountain behind.

There is rock in the frames. Rock like frost would have been on the pane, or faces steaming on the glass.

"What did you get up to today?" Peter asks, mopping up the gravy on his plate with a chunk of bread.

"Nothing much," Anne says, sucking on a chicken wing.

It would take too long to explain. She will tell him eventually And he will believe, mistakenly, that the day had been too unimportant to mention at the time. She will tell him one day, inadvertently.

FIRST THINGS FIRST

NEXT TIME, IF I GET THE CHANCE, I'll ask more questions first. I imagine some kind of questionnaire. A snappy little quiz to hand out at the bedroom door. It seems there are always some subjects you just never get around to until the whole situation is pretty far advanced. And then it always turns out that those were the important things. The ones you should have known about right from the start.

First things first.

QUESTION ONE: *Are you allergic to cats?*

I come from a long line of cats. I was only five when I made the major discovery that, at any given time, there are any number of stray cats just roaming around out there free for the taking. My mother, I realize now, withstood this barrage of skinny furry (and probably wormy) creatures remarkably well, and we always had at least one cat around the house. Occasionally she tried to talk me out of it by explaining how maybe some other family owned the cat and they would be missing it terribly and crying. But I was young and had no sympathy for people who lost things.

When I figured she was getting fed up with me and might give me trouble, I would run home from school carrying a cat under one arm like a football, toss it in the back door, and keep on running. I went down the street to the park where I would swing furiously for half an hour while the cat, I hoped, was making itself at home. If, when I did venture back to the house, there was a dish of milk by the fridge and my mother was talking to the cat while she started supper, I knew we were all set. My father was always the one who got sent out for more kitty litter.

But all my cats were short-lived. The world, it seemed, was rife with things that killed cats. Dogs, fish-hooks, rotten meat, distemper, and speeding cars that didn't stop. Finally, my mother decided that neither of us could take much more of this. So my father rigged up a leash on the clothesline for the next cat which turned out to be a big orange tom I called Punky.

One night that summer I slept over at my friend Ellen's house. It was too hot to sleep so we spent the whole night with a flashlight under the covers reading *True Story* and touching ourselves. Ellen stole the magazines from the drugstore where my mother worked. When I got home in the morning my mother was sitting on the back step crying and my father was watering the garden, something he usually never did. My mother said the cat was dead, had hung himself in the maple tree while trying to catch a bird. Instinctively I knew this was some cruel and unusual punishment for the feeling that came from reading *True Story*.

Right now I have only one cat because I live in a miniature basement suite. Her name is Jessie. Sometimes I call her Liz Taylor. She's black, fat, and very sure of herself. In the sunlight her fur shines blue. Some people say I'm neurotic (or at least very odd) about my cat but I don't care. There have been so many times when she was all I had. So now my cat collection consists mostly of cats on calendars, cats on posters, and cats hand-painted on little ceramic boxes. I also have Polaroid pictures of Jessie taped all over the fridge door. Love me, love my cat.

Last April I met this guy James at the horseshoe tournament.

Half the town was there with all their kids and all their dogs, no cats of course. Cats never get to go anywhere.

James started talking to me during the ladies' final. He said he'd been wanting to meet me for weeks.

And then he said, "Joyce, do you ever think you're more clever than your friends?"

I thought that was very perceptive of him because maybe, just maybe, sometimes I do. So I started paying more attention to his good brown skin, his curly black hair, and the long muscles in his thighs. He told me he was reading *War and Peace* for the third time.

James kept bringing me more cold beer from the ice-filled bathtub in the garage. Another woman, Lana, kept bringing *him* beer and hovering, but he just kept touching my arm and asking me who my favorite writer was. It was all wonderfully tense. I must admit that sometimes I like that sort of thing. But only if I'm winning.

Later it turned out that Lana was his lover right before me. But you can't always know these things at the time.

When it got dark, those few of us who were still hanging around went into the house and arranged ourselves on and around a sagging old couch. I remember it was the color of dried blood. Lana sat on one arm and it fell off. We all laughed warmly to let her know such minor disgraces didn't matter to us. James played the mandolin and sang. There were also some guitars and pretty soon we were all singing. I thought about how James and I could be together and talk about music and books all the time. Sometimes we would play backgammon and have liqueurs in our coffee. I would show him some of the stories I've written and then he would sing to me. A Bob Dylan song.

When I finally got tired of waiting for something more to happen and got up to leave, James said, "Joyce, I want to start seeing more of you." I was ready for anything.

He started phoning and coming over to my apartment, sometimes for supper. I quickly discovered that he favored romaine lettuce, baked salmon and seedless green grapes. I suspected that he'd never once succumbed to the glory of greasy french fries. When he was fasting, which was at least once a week, he drank gallons of ice water and nothing else. I admired his willpower but had no particular use for it myself. He lent me his favorite book, a scathing exposé of the eating habits of North Americans.

He was working extra shifts at the sawmill and never had much free time. He started coming over late at night without warning. I had no idea when to expect him. Sometimes when he arrived I was already in bed, reading or asleep with the cat on my chest. Other times I sat at the kitchen table until two in the morning, all dressed and casually keeping the coffee warm. Somewhere I'd already learned or been told that phoning a new man too often or asking for more information was unpleasant. And I already knew that expecting too much from James was risky; he couldn't take the pressure. I was always perfecting my technique of biding my time.

When James did appear at the door, he'd start grabbing at me as soon as he could get his work boots off. He smelled like freshly-cut wood. (Afterwards, I wondered if maybe it was really some racy new aftershave designed to make women drool for the I'm-a-labourer look.)

He never actually pushed me into the bedroom but he was always spinning me around and pointing me in the right direction. Pin the tail on the donkey.

I just assumed that we'd get around to all those other things, the music and the books and the all-night discussions, soon enough.

But there was a problem with the cat. Every time we had sex, first I had to lie in bed waiting and trying to look voluptuous while James gobbled four or five antihistamines and gagged.

Jessie always sleeps on the bed no matter who else happens to be in it. Then, the whole time, while I wiggled around underneath James looking for the right spot, he snuffled and choked and cursed the cat. Afterwards, he had to get dressed right away and go home before his eyes swelled shut. He told me I'd have to get rid of the cat. Jessie, of course, adored him.

One night when he was trying to get my nightgown off, something occurred to me. I said, "What makes you think you can come over here and climb into bed with me anytime you feel like it?" He'd run out of antihistamines that night anyway. And I wouldn't give my cat away for anybody.

James, I suppose, was one of those guys that afterwards you can't imagine what you ever saw in him and you feel like a damn fool. And your friends all tell you they never liked him anyway but they didn't say anything before because they didn't want to hurt your feelings. And you wonder why nobody ever tells you the truth until it's too late to save you.

QUESTION TWO: *Do you sleep on the couch every night after supper?*

When I lived at home, the same thing happened every night. While my mother and I were still sitting at the table having our second cup of tea, my father would head into the living room aimed at the couch. He snored while we cleared up the supper dishes. Some nights he slept there right through till the eleven o'clock news. We were all in the living room and I was reading something for school and my mother was sewing or working on her stamp collection and watching TV at the same time. My father slept on the couch in his white teeshirt and green work pants, snoring with his mouth open, bubbling a bit, and heaving around. I couldn't even look at him.

My mother often said she hadn't slept in the daytime for years. From that I figured women were just naturally better than men because they didn't need to sleep so much.

Last August I met this guy Dean at a party. I remember thinking he looked a little tired but I didn't see that as a serious problem at the time. He fell asleep at the party but then we'd all had quite a bit to drink and he wasn't the only one. He looked like a child when he was asleep. It wasn't until later that I discovered this is true of many people and is not an accurate measure of one's character.

Dean came over for supper twice the first week. He arrived right after work, armed with a bottle of good red wine and a new shirt. He seemed so hurt if I didn't kiss him passionately at the door and then rush right off to open the wine. I thought this was substantial proof of how much he loved me already. I served the wine in my good crystal glasses. Long-stemmed, they made me think of roses.

After supper then he wanted me to lie down with him but it wasn't for sleeping yet. I liked that (he called it "dessert") but it wasn't always so much fun on a full stomach.

Once, at exactly the wrong moment, he said, "Don't make so much noise."

After that I couldn't work up as much enthusiasm anymore.

Dean talked a lot about moving back to Ontario where he owned sixty acres and building a house together. He said it could be done for $5000. I thought he was being overly optimistic but it wasn't until later that I felt compelled to point this out to him. He said we would have chickens, a cow, a big garden, and some babies.

I began to indulge myself in sunny fantasies. It was always summer on our farm but if winter ever did come, we would spend the evenings reading by the fireplace, making popcorn, and touching each other every now and then. I imagined working in the big garden, pregnant in a long flowered dress, weeding the potatoes with a smiling little round person (male or female, it didn't matter which) crawling down the row behind me. Someone I know now would arrive for an unexpected visit and go away in a week quite miserable with envy.

By the third week, Dean was coming over every day at five-thirty on the dot, wondering what was for supper. He still got a passionate kiss at the door but he didn't bring me the wine anymore. (I can see now that I wasn't paying enough attention to detail at the time.) I didn't mind the cooking every night. I must admit I like to cook. Dean's favorite food was spaghetti. Somehow all that chopping and spicing and tasting convinced me that I loved him as much as he loved me.

By the fourth week, he still wanted my spaghetti but now every night after supper he would flop down on the couch and say, "I just need to relax for a few minutes." Sometimes he even asked for a blanket. Then he slept for three or four hours. I can't say as how I found this very entertaining.

One day he went to sleep on the couch *before* supper and I realized he'd been lying to me all along — he slept so much that he'd never have time to do anything, let alone build a house and help me in the big garden too. I also remembered that I don't like farms.

I kept stirring and tasting the spaghetti sauce until I could hear Dean snoring. Then I switched everything off, left the pasta to congeal, and walked over to the ballpark. There was no game that night. I sat at the very top of the bleachers and spit sunflower seeds all over the bottom seats. The base lines had been freshly chalked, the infield raked, and the backboard repainted. There was a district tournament coming up on the weekend. The mosquitoes were bad but I sat there until it got dark and then I took my own sweet time strolling back to the house.

Dean was still sleeping, the cat was outside, and the whole house reeked of garlic.

It was something of an anti-climax. I was looking for a fight.

Some people have heard all about my mother too. Back in high school, I went out for a while with a guy named Ted. He was the first boyfriend I had who owned a car. On Friday nights, after an hour or two at Country Style Donuts, he'd drive me out to the airport parking lot, our industrialized version of the old lover's lane. While he kissed me and tried to put his tongue in my ear, I gabbed on about my mother. Instinctively I knew that even by proxy, her image could protect me from doing something I didn't want to, something which it was no longer necessary or feasible to refuse on strictly moral grounds. Winter was coming and we had to leave the car running. I knew this was dangerous too. One night, after a few weeks of this, Ted suggested we go over to his house and take all our clothes off. He said we would sit around in the nude and drink hot rum toddies. I had no idea what I would talk about while sitting in the nude — certainly not my mother. Maybe we would compare scars. I never went.

Just after Christmas last year, I went out with this guy Larry who, as it turned out, was always talking about his wonderful mother and his awful ex-wife.

I first met Larry when he was singing in the Landmark Lounge here in town. That very first night he struck me as being kind of soft and sad, nervous but pretending not to be. I must admit that sometimes I go for that type. I have occasional spells of wanting to be somebody's mother.

Larry was wearing blue velvet pants and a silk shirt embroidered with blue fish. He was very thin. His hair was pale red, long at the sides and thinning on top. Under the bright stage lights, his face and hair were all one color. He was attractive though, with a gravelly voice and acrobat fingers on his electric guitar. All the other women in the bar were obviously admiring him so I did too. Pretty soon he was looking right back at me and I imagined he was singing those sweet songs to me. I sent him up a rum and Coke and he came right over to my table when he finished singing.

Pretty soon Larry was staying at my place whenever he was singing in town, and phoning me every other night when he was out on the road.

Sometimes I drove out to spend the weekend with Larry wherever he happened to be playing. Usually we could have a free room in the hotel. These rooms were all the same, the sheets were always yellow, and the toilet was always running. On the Saturday we would go out in the afternoon and wander through these strange towns, shopping and taking pictures of old buildings. Larry took pictures of everything, especially me.

On the Saturday night I'd go down to the bar where Larry was singing and sit all alone, nursing my Scotch and concentrating on looking cold and mysterious. I liked to watch the young girls all admiring him up there on the stage. I smiled serenely while they sent him up drinks and little notes scribbled on paper napkins and empty cigarette packages. He saved the notes and read them to me later in bed. They were so in awe of him and offered phone numbers, drinks, kisses, true love. We made fun of their fantasies. Only I knew he was wearing his white Stanfields under his velvet pants. He collected the notes in an old spiral scrapbook but I never doubted him. Usually we spent Sunday lying around the hotel room, admiring ourselves and feeling safe and smug.

Beside Larry, I became tough and large. I wanted to look after him, save him from suffering anything ever again. This included colds, TV dinners, and another broken heart. He adored me. Once he said, "Joyce, there's not one thing about you that I don't like." With a rush of recognition, I understood that I'd been waiting to hear that from someone for years.

He told me first thing that he'd been married before. His

divorce had become final a month before he met me. For a long time he didn't call her by name, only "my ex-wife" or "that bitch." She'd left him without warning, taken the kids and moved back in with her parents who were rich and lived in a monstrous mansion in North Vancouver. Larry said it was all their fault, they'd never liked him and they turned her against him. They wouldn't let him see his own kids. He made it sound like a conspiracy.

He often said, "I gave her everything she asked for and then she left me anyway."

This was supposed to make me feel sorry for him and sometimes it did.

But he thought his mother was perfect. Her name was Irene. In various anecdotes, Irene was wise, beautiful, patient, understanding, strong, and she made the world's best scalloped potatoes. I just knew I was never going to turn out to be that good. I was doomed.

Of all the things I ever cooked for him, the only thing Larry ever paid attention to was the scalloped potatoes. I vaguely recall some passing remark about a big pot of meatless minestrone (we were dabbling in vegetarianism then, exploring the secret world of lentils, eggplant, and crunchy granola) but I can't remember now whether he did or didn't like it. Larry was the most timid eater I've ever met. He picked through each meal like he was looking for little bugs or hairs. He chewed like a rabbit, only with his front teeth because his back teeth were rotten.

This was because, when he was a kid, his mother didn't have enough money to take him to the dentist. She raised Larry all by herself because her husband had turned out to be a rat and a petty thief who left them when Larry was just a baby. Larry made their poverty sound splendid. About his father, he said, "We never needed him anyway, we were better off without him." And I could see that he hated him.

Larry's ex-wife's name was Janet and pretty soon she was getting blamed for everything that went wrong. Whenever I criticized Larry, he said, "It's all Janet's fault, she made me that way."

Whenever, in a rush of guilty affection, I told him he was the best man in the whole world, he said, "You'll have to thank my mother for that, she made me that way."

Between Janet and Irene, I couldn't figure out who I was supposed to be. He already had one woman to hate and another to love. What did he need me for anyway? Perhaps he thought of me as a captive audience.

Over the years, he'd built himself up a whole bank of debits and credits. On the one hand, he would stroke lovingly for me the acute memory of his mother waiting at the corner to walk him home from school every day. They couldn't afford to move to a safer section of town. On the other hand, he would relive vividly for me the time he came home from two weeks on the road and found Janet in bed with his best friend. "In *my* bed," he wept. In the final analysis, this trespass seemed the worst part of it.

Once, feeling a little drunk and perversely intimate, I attempted to reciprocate and confessed to him my entire love life thus far. He never forgave me.

One night when Larry was out on the road, I went to the lounge and got drunk and spent the night with a guy named Sam. The next morning, changing the sheets, I realized I could be just as unlovable as the next (or the last) person. I'd always felt obligated to be a good person. The realization that I didn't have to be was maybe not something you'd especially want to know, but it was a relief just the same. I gave up trying to feel guilty and went to the laundromat.

Larry came home a week later and I told him about Sam. I knew that, as far as Larry was concerned, I'd already done the worst thing possible and there was no turning back now.

He punched the wall and cried while I flew at him like a bird against a picture window. Finally I said, "Now I can see why your wife left you." I guess I'd always known I'd be able to use that on him one day — just because he was always using it on me. He'd always acted as though that was the only interesting thing about him — the fact that Janet had left him and so, naturally, he was scarred for life.

THE FOURTH AND FINAL QUESTION: *If you're not looking for love, then what are you looking for anyway?*

It seems that nobody wants to believe in love anymore. Certainly nobody wants to admit that's what they'd really like to find out of all this rushing around. I wonder how everybody got to be so afraid.

I used to think it would all get easier as I got older. But I can see now that it only gets harder. And so many of the things you discover about people just by wanting or trying to love them turn out to be things you were happier not knowing. Too much water under the bridge.

I used to think I would die without love. Now I know that's not true. Usually this knowledge reassures me but sometimes even now I catch myself wishing I still believed it. Wishing my heart would stay broken just once. Broken and bleeding, a stain to scare strangers away.

But I know now that love can't keep you alive.

I was still in high school, cultivating a crush on a boy named Don who was three grades older than me. I knew he had a girlfriend who went to a school across town but I figured I could work around that. One day Don skipped school to go fishing with two friends at Indian Lake. They were drunk in the boat and when it went over, Don drowned. The other two lived. One moved away to Winnipeg with his family and I heard that the other one rushed right out and married a girl I never liked.

There was something shameful about dying when you were skipping school and drunk too. None of us talked about it much. Death by drowning was no distinction. It only meant that I could never dream about Don anymore without having silver gills appear somewhere around his ears. And it also meant there could never be a reason to stop loving him.

Anyway, I guess you might think from what I've told you that I'm not very good at this sort of thing. I don't think it's my fault though. It just seems that all the men I meet start out one way and end up another. Next time, if I get the chance, I'll ask more questions first.

TRUE OR FALSE

MAVIS SINGER IS SITTING out on the back patio reading *The National Enquirer* just for a few minutes while there's no one around likely to catch her. Waiting for last night's supper dishes to cool off in the dishwasher, she's letting the June sun dry her hair. It's grown back some now but it's still pretty short and shaggy-looking, which, fortunately, is the style this year. Purple is the color this summer so Mavis' sun-dress is purple. In this position, stretched out in the canary yellow (last summer's color but passable this year as well) canvas lawn chair, Mavis looks pregnant but isn't.

The house behind her, financed largely by the insurance money, is breezy-looking, a curious cool blue with white trim. It is an old house made over inside and out, as is the emerging pattern in this part of the city. Everything around her is brilliant and acute — geraniums, greenhouse, garbage cans, picket fence, colors blatant and blazing in the heat. It's nearly noon but there's nothing to get in a hurry about — she's got all day. It's Wednesday. The neighborhood kids are coming home for lunch all up and down the block, zipping through the alley on their bicycles, rearing up on them as if they were stallions, glinting electrically in the sunlight.

Suddenly one boy, who is carrying a big bag of peaches under one arm, rides his bike right into the side of the garbage truck which has been lumbering from house to house and is now directly behind Mavis' place. She leaps out of the lawn chair and runs to the boy who lies curled on his side, half on the

123

gravel and half in her backyard. The peaches are rolling away in all directions like marbles or pearls from a broken strand.

TRUE OR FALSE?

FALSE.

Mavis leaps out of the lawn chair and runs into the house, into the kitchen which is modern and cool. She squats down in front of the refrigerator, leaning her forehead against its cold green door, holding her stomach, praying, hating herself but praying for forgiveness just the same. Bravery, she realizes, is admirable but no longer possible.

Mavis looks pregnant and might be. She isn't really worried one way or the other. Where she comes from, these things are, if not exactly taken for granted, then certainly taken in stride.

*

For as long as Mavis Clay could remember there was always a summer fair in Indian Mound. It was held the last weekend of August in the open field just east of town which must have been owned by somebody but was never used for anything else. The dilapidated barn in the middle became the exhibition hall, crammed full of Indian Mound matrons in flowered dresses fanning themselves with newspapers and examining the prize-winning beets, pies, peach preserves, and afghans. To the right of the barn, where all the cars were parked, the little kids could play horseshoes or go for free pony rides. To the left were the smaller livestock barns and the performing ring.

Mavis went to the fair every year just because it was something to do for a day at the end of the long hot vacant summer. That particular summer, when Mavis was fifteen, she went to the fair alone and ignored everybody she knew. She hadn't been home for a couple of days but she figured the family probably hadn't missed her much, there were so many of them. They were all there (except for her oldest brother, Jack, who was already in jail) plus a whole parcel of relatives, some from out of town even, come to make their annual visit to Indian Mound, rather like paying your respects. But Mavis ignored them all, even her little sister Beth who clearly adored her and kept waving madly in her direction.

Mavis stood with her back to all of them where they sat, squinting and sweating, ranged in lawn chairs and on upside-down milk cans along the side of the pig barn. She was watching her best friend Molly Florence on her horse Starr in the first round of the barrel-racing. She was sucking on an ice cream cone in her new blue short-shorts and her white sandals. Her hair in a pony tail straight down her back felt silky in the sunlight, her skin in the heat felt succulent.

Suddenly two German Shepherds ran into the ring, snarling and chewing at each other's throats. Starr pranced sideways and then reared up, throwing Molly to the ground. Snorting and bucking, the horse came right at Mavis who did not move a muscle. Some man grabbed her by the hair, snapping her head back, and yanked her out of the way just as the horse plunged headfirst screaming into the dirt right where Mavis had stood. Molly lay curled in the middle of ring as the two dogs rolled around in the mud beside her and people came running from all directions.

Mavis wandered away across the field, past the barn, and perched on the hot hood of somebody's car to watch the little kids riding around in circles on those gentle fat ponies. As it turned out, Molly wasn't seriously hurt — a broken leg was all. Mr. Florence shot the damn horse.

TRUE OR FALSE?

TRUE.

Accidents will happen.

For Mavis, it was the kind of day that later you go over and over again in your mind, looking for clues, and still later you find yourself running face-first into parts of it, patches or chunks of it, at inappropriate moments. It was the kind of day that has nothing to do with anything else but itself . . . the kind of day that marks both the end and the beginning of something . . . the beginning of living dangerously, yes, but the end of what?

*

Just after lunch (herbed cream cheese and Hungarian salami on a toasted bagel), Mavis Singer walks the four blocks east to Murphy's Corner Grocery. She is careful to lock and double-check the door behind her. There are starting to be more and more burglaries in the neighborhood and Mavis is afraid of being robbed, afraid of losing all her treasures again. The back alley is empty, unchanged, as if nothing has happened. Maybe Mavis can believe that nothing did.

Usually Mavis goes to the Safeway at Chesterfield Mall but she only needs a few things today. To tell the truth, she secretly prefers Murphy's anyway, partly because her best friend Tess Berry shops there and partly because of the store itself, which is dimly-lit and jumbled, in an old-fashioned way, aromatic, with the barley, brown rice and other grains stored in big red barrels in the back corner. They do not carry Kraft Dinner, Sara Lee cakes or Coke. Murphy, if there is such a person, is long gone — to the country, Mavis assumes, the grave, or the bank. The clerks and the stock boys are all foreigners, transplanted from tiny humid overpopulated countries, striking Mavis as loyal, sincere and happy to be here.

TRUE OR FALSE?

TRUE.

Mavis is secretly overwhelmed by the vast selection at the Safeway and when the cute little checkout girl says, "Have a nice day!", Mavis only nods grimly, knowing that she says the same thing to everyone and wanting to tell her to suck eggs.

*

When Mavis Clay was sixteen, she was involved in a serious single-car accident on the Old Post Road one August night. She and Molly Florence were cruising the countryside with two Indian Mound brothers, Zack and Bub Hammer, Mavis in the front seat with Bub and Molly in the back with Zack, a mutually-satisfactory arrangement the two girls had decided on in the Rainbow Café before ever getting into the car.

The car went out of control for no apparent reason, rolled three times and came to rest on its roof in an irrigation ditch. Molly and Zack were shaken up and bruised but not badly hurt, so Zack ran back down the road for help while Molly stayed with Mavis and Bub. They had both gone through the windshield and lay crumpled together in the rotten water, the single intact headlight shining right on them and the radio still playing. Molly got down in the ditch with them and held their heads and sang silly songs in a crying crooning whine until the ambulance came. When the police arrived, there was some question about drinking and driving but, as it turned out, Bub Hammer lost the sight in his left eye and that, it seemed, was punishment enough — no charges were ever laid. Both he and Mavis were in the hospital for weeks. The doctors assured Mavis that the scars on her face would disappear in time. They said she was damn lucky to be alive.

When Mavis Clay was sixteen, she nearly died.

TRUE OR FALSE?

FALSE.

This is a carefully-constructed story that Mavis Singer wants her new friends to believe because she thinks it makes her somehow more valuable, more precious to them.

What really happened was that Mavis got disgustingly drunk at Molly Florence's sixteenth birthday party and fell or walked through the picture window of Molly's parents' house. She lay face-down on the lawn in limbo until somebody found her and drove her to the hospital. The blood and the dew on her face were both wet, one warm, one cool, both wet, the same only different. And Bub Hammer lost his left eye in a barroom brawl.

When the bandages were finally unravelled and removed, Mavis was, more than anything, surprised. The disfigurement wasn't that extreme, not grotesque or repulsive or anything like that. She thought she could even grow fond of the scars someday, take a kind of perverse pride in them eventually. They were like trophies, tangible proof of something . . . pain, survival . . . mortality or immortality or both.

The scars did fade with the years, as the doctors had promised, and now they are like lace or slugs, depending on the light and her frame of mind.

*

When the phone rings the first time it is Molly from Indian Mound, who lives in the city now too, in a low-income housing project with her husband, one-eyed Bub Hammer, and their two kids. She works sporadically as a bun-wrapper in a bakery downtown. Molly and Mavis used to write back and forth a lot when Molly and Bub were still living in Indian Mound but they seldom see each other now. Molly, who has always been a loyal sort of woman, is constantly calling to suggest they get together for lunch, coffee, bingo, but Mavis always puts her off. Today Molly wants to go over to Chesterfield Mall and shop around. Mavis, who is defrosting the fridge and feeling mildly irritated,

says, "You wouldn't know me if you knew me now," and rips
the telephone out of the wall, for once and for all.

TRUE OR FALSE?

FALSE.

This is what Mavis, who really is defrosting the fridge and
feeling mildly irritated, would like to say and do. Instead, she
says, "Oh, I can't today, Molly, I'm expecting the TV repairman
this afternoon," crossing her fingers behind her back. The TV
set works fine — for a thousand bucks it should. Then the two
women talk affably for a few minutes about the transit strike,
their folks back in Indian Mound and, of course, the indecent
heat. They talk just long enough so that Mavis can hang up
gracefully and not feel guilty about it.

*

Mavis Clay could usually count on running into Danny Singer
at the Rainbow Café. She and Molly and the rest of the crowd
hung out there all summer, pumping coins into the table-side
jukeboxes, slurping up milkshakes and chips and gravy. Usually
Danny would slide silently in beside Mavis in their booth.
Sometimes he parked his convertible right in front of the café
and he and Mavis would go out and lounge against it for a
while. This was when Molly would disappear — she wasn't
stupid, she knew when she wasn't needed or wanted around
anymore. She knew when to leave them alone, those two . . .
Danny in his cowboy boots and jeans, a pack of cigarettes stuffed
up the sleeve of his black teeshirt . . . Mavis in love.

Danny was quite a few years older than Mavis and worked
pumping gas at the Indian Mound Esso. His family had a pig
farm just west of town but it was never really clear where
Danny lived. He was liable to turn up anywhere in that

wonderful car, drinking a beer. Mavis knew that sometimes, when the weather was bad, he rented a room for a week or so upstairs at the Indian Mound Hotel. She suspected that the rest of the time he slept in the car. She loved this about him, this unanchored itinerant quality. He could go anywhere, do anything; he could take care of himself.

To tell the truth, Danny Singer was the only guy that Mavis had ever really wanted. Secretly, hugging herself, she thought of him as "forbidden fruit" . . . something tropical, succulent and potent, slightly bruised, possibly poisonous. He was a vagabond living just this side of the law. Mavis had no reason to suspect that he would ever change.

TRUE OR FALSE?

TRUE.

How was she supposed to know that Danny Singer would gain weight, lose his tan and some of his hair, take up bowling and stamp collecting, quit drinking, send his aging parents to a retirement village in Florida, fall in love with mowing the lawn, trade the convertible in on a station wagon? How was she supposed to know that Danny would mutate into the perfect husband, the perfect father, the perfect Little League baseball coach?

*

When the phone rings the second time it is Tess Berry, Mavis' best friend. She teaches the watercolor class which Mavis attends every Thursday night at the art college and is, of course, tall and slim and intense with long curly black hair and wild-looking eyes. Having travelled extensively, now she dresses in elegant, inspired outfits picked up for a pittance on other continents — Asia, Africa, South America. At various times in the past, Tess has experimented with photography, body-building and cocaine. Now she writes poetry, plays the mandolin, raises doves, sculpts, and grows her own herbs. Except for Mavis, the crowd Tess travels with is composed exclusively of painters, playwrights, sculptors, poets, actors and musicians. Her husband Russell is an actor and a good one at that. They do not plan to have children.

Today Tess and Mavis make plans to drive to class together tomorrow night. Afterwards they will go for a couple of drinks at The Black Cat, a jazz club, one of those new hybrids, the deli/bar, which are springing up in the more fashionable neighborhoods around the city. Mavis finds such clubs convenient because now she can say, "I'm going to the deli," when what she really means is, "I'm going to the bar," a more determined and dangerous announcement somehow, one more likely to meet with resistance.

Mavis prolongs the telephone conversation as long as is casually possible, telling Tess about the accident in the alley, how the peaches went rolling every which way, how she ran out to help that poor careless child. Mavis is flattered by this friendship with Tess who, she imagines, has no doubts about herself and no secrets either. Tess is everything that Mavis wants to be.

TRUE OR FALSE?

TRUE.

Tess is everything that Mavis wants to be now.

*

Mavis Clay and Danny Singer were getting more and more restless while everyone else in Indian Mound got more and more sluggish, lazier and lazier as that relentless suffocating summer wore on. Existing for weeks in a sulky state of perpetual excitement, they were looking for adventure, whatever came their way, planning their escapade in endless and abundant detail.

Mavis only went home when she felt like it, to grab a change of clothes or a half-decent meal, home where they usually said, "At least you're not pregnant," or "At least you're not in jail," and then went on about their business. Mavis' parents had other things to worry about, what with that tribe of hellions they'd managed to bring into the world. Mavis figured that another body more or less in that zoo didn't make much difference and she was probably right. Every time she did go back to the farm there was a different brother or sister sleeping in her bed anyway. Most of the time she stayed with Danny, in the car or in his room at the hotel.

One morning Danny said, "I can't stand it one more minute," so they packed up the convertible and drove to a public beach about forty miles west, Deadman's Point, where they spent the afternoon in and out of the shallow water, drinking beer and collecting shells. It wasn't until the next morning, after spending the night at Deadman's and then heading west again instead of turning around and going back to Indian Mound, that Mavis realized they were really doing it this time.

They made their way across the prairies, pretending to be tourists, sleeping in the car, sometimes in a cheap motel. Mavis had no idea where Danny got the money and she didn't like to ask. They ended up in Euclid, Alberta, because the place where they stopped for gas needed a mechanic.

Pretending to be married, they lived together in two rooms in back of the station, sleeping on a mattress on the floor and cooking their meals on the grill in the restaurant out front. Mavis helped out in the restaurant when it got busy, dishing up endless pork chops, mashed potatoes and hot rhubarb pie to punks and truckers. Some of the girls who came in tried to make friends, but Mavis ignored their overtures, figuring that she already knew enough people to do her for a while. She and Danny kept to themselves. These girls struck her as too innocent, too eager anyway, and certainly untrustworthy. She was always feeling crabby and her feet were just killing her but she made better tips if she smiled and winked and bent over a lot when she cleaned tables.

By November Mavis knew she was pregnant but she figured that if she just ignored it, it would go away by itself, like the flu or a mosquito in the bedroom in the dark. Mavis wasn't stupid, she knew this couldn't really happen, but still . . .

One day she took all her tip money out of the jar and caught the bus back to Indian Mound. The driver dropped her off at the side of the highway because the town was too small to be a regular stop. She was scared to death.

TRUE OR FALSE?

FALSE.

Mavis was bored to death. Euclid by this time had become just like Indian Mound, except that it was hillier and she didn't know anybody there but the kind old couple who owned the station. Once they'd got there it seemed as if Danny's sense of adventure had just dried right up.

The gossip stirred up by Mavis' return to Indian Mound alone was scant substitute for the initial intoxication of their escapade, but it was better than nothing. Even that didn't last long though, as the townspeople quickly forgot about her and got busy with Christmas. Only Molly was interested in all the juicy details.

*

When the phone rings a third time, it is probably either Molly again, the doctor calling about Mavis' Monday appointment, or a wrong number. Mavis, who is cutting back the spider plant, just lets it ring.

TRUE OR FALSE?

TRUE.

Mavis lets the phone ring and ring until the fool on the other end finally gives up. This makes her feel gaily indifferent and powerful too.

*

Danny Singer was no dummy: he went back to Indian Mound too, but not for another month or so, until he'd given Mavis some time to think about it.

Mavis and Danny were married in a simple ceremony in the Indian Mound Church in January. Molly Florence was maid of honor and one of the bride's older brothers, John Allan, stood up for Danny. The bride wore a knee-length white dress which caused a minor flurry of interest. Both sets of parents disapproved of the marriage but had resigned themselves to the fact that there was nothing else to be done. The wedding dance was held in the Legion basement and everybody had a good time in spite of themselves.

With Danny's savings (which were far more than Mavis or anyone else would ever have guessed), they bought a small old house on Main Street. Danny got his old job back at the Indian Mound Esso, where he was quickly promoted to head mechanic. Mavis fell easily into the role of young housewife, spending her days sewing curtains and slipcovers, fixing up the nursery, planning a garden, and cooking good nutritious dinners for Danny every night. Danny bought Mavis a blue budgie for her nineteenth birthday, to keep her company, he said, until the baby was born. Mavis, who would have preferred a fluffy white kitten or a horse but didn't like to complain, named the bird Julie. The baby, a girl they named Amy, was born in June, barely six months after the wedding, thus satisfying everybody's suspicions. They were making improvements on the old house while saving up their money to buy a new one and Danny was nursing his dream of owning the Indian Mound Esso himself someday.

For a few years, Mavis, Danny and little Amy Singer lived quietly and happily in the little house on Main Street.

TRUE OR FALSE?

TRUE.

For a few years, the young Singer family threatened to live happily ever after and disappoint everyone.

*

Mavis Singer is having her afternoon nap, a secret indulgence she feels guilty about but just can't give up yet. In the dream Amy is riding a black horse on a beach. The horse bursts into flames and runs into the water which is a hundred feet deep. Danny is trapped under somebody's car and can't save her. Mavis is afraid of fire and has forgotten how to swim. In the dream there is no sound.

TRUE OR FALSE?

TRUE.

The dream disturbs Mavis for the rest of the day.

*

One morning just before Amy's fifth birthday Mavis took $100 from Danny's sock drawer (she called this borrowing, not stealing, because after all they were married), got Amy all dressed and caught a bus back to Euclid, Alberta. The old couple who owned the gas station was still there and Mavis got work in the restaurant again. The suite in back was occupied so Mavis took a room in a boarding house just until she could afford something better.

Back in Indian Mound, rumour had it that an older man, a married man named Joe Fletcher, was involved. Joe had disappeared at about the same time, went out for a loaf of bread and never came back.

TRUE OR FALSE?

FALSE.

Joe's disappearance at the same time was just a coincidence. He went east, not west, and, as it turned out, came slinking back to Indian Mound three months later, tail between his legs.

Danny Singer was no dummy and when he tracked Mavis down back in Euclid, she was at the laundromat, folding clothes and reading *The National Enquirer* while Amy played with her dolls on the floor.

*

Mavis is out working in the garden, sweating and hacking worms in half with the hoe.

TRUE OR FALSE?

TRUE.

Mavis hates worms, even though she knows they're good for the soil. Mavis hates the garden, which was not her idea in the first place, because it reminds her of Indian Mound and the old house on Main Street. There are some things that can no longer be thought about.

*

Back in Indian Mound, Mavis and Danny began saving their money in earnest. They'd had about all they could take and wanted to buy a house in the city. They went in most weekends all through that boring summer, just checking it out, and by the end of August they knew exactly what they wanted, which is more than most people can say.

Danny was working all the time, ten or twelve hours a day, six or seven days a week, and Mavis was spending a lot of time over at Molly's, who was married now too, to Bub Hammer, and living right across the street. They had coffee together most days, at one house or the other.

One afternoon, after Mavis had put Amy down for her nap, she wandered across the street to Molly's just for a few minutes. This day it was too hot for coffee, too humid to sit inside that little hotbox of a house, so they were having a beer in the backyard, admiring the garden and the gladiolas and whining about the heat, when all of a sudden the fire siren went off, freezing activity all over town, curdling Mavis' stomach just like it always did. The one thing she was most afraid of was fire.

It took Mavis only a minute to realize that it was *her* house that was on fire. She was up and running, screaming, and before anyone could stop her, she was inside the burning house, inside the flames, flailing through the smoke to Amy, coming back out through the picture window that had exploded, her hair ablaze and the child lying limp in her arms as if she were already dead.

TRUE OR FALSE?

TRUE.

The house was reduced to a smoking black skeleton, faulty wiring, all of their accumulated treasures lost. Poor Julie, the budgie, was cooked in her cage, so much roast meat, and all of Mavis' beautiful hair was burnt off. The insurance money would enable them to move to the city sooner than anticipated but, of course, they weren't thinking about that yet. Mavis knew that she and Amy both were lucky to be alive. Afterwards, when people went on and on about her bravery, she felt hazy and surprised. Brave is not something you think of yourself as being.

*

Mavis is in the kitchen starting supper when Amy gets home from school and Danny gets home from work. Amy's books and lunchbox, Danny's boots and coveralls, all drop in a heap beside the back door. He is co-owner of a garage down on East 27th now. He's handing Mavis a peach he found lying in the backyard so she tells him the story of the accident, the true story. Danny is understanding, comforting, he puts an arm around her shoulders, rests his cheek on the top of her head. He knows everything about her by now. There are no secrets, no surprises, between them. Anything can be discussed, examined, dealt with maturely. Amy is in the living room watching reruns of *Mister Ed, The Talking Horse*.

After supper, the Singer family will have a quick game of Old Maid which is Amy's favorite. Then Mavis and Danny will do the dishes, she washes, he dries and puts away, and talk about Amy's eighth birthday party coming up on Saturday. Amy has already invited all her little friends from school. Mavis decides that a barbecue, just burgers and dogs, would be the best idea. Danny will go out and mow the lawn while Mavis helps Amy with her homework, runs her bath and then tucks her into bed. Then Mavis and Danny will watch the early movie and go to bed right after the news.

TRUE OR FALSE?

TRUE.

After supper, all of these things will happen and the Singer family will sleep peacefully all night long in their cool blue house, as if they've been doing it all their lives.

TRUE OR FALSE?

FALSE.

After supper, Mavis Singer will go down to The Black Cat Deli/Bar with Tess Barry and pick up some young guy in leather pants and spend the night at his place.

TRUE OR FALSE?

FALSE.

After supper, Amy Singer will accidentally electrocute herself with the curling iron in the bathtub.

TRUE OR FALSE?

FALSE.

After supper, Danny Singer will go and visit Molly Hammer from Indian Mound, with whom he is having an affair.

TRUE OR FALSE?

FALSE.

After supper, Mavis Singer will go and visit Bub Hammer from Indian Mound, with whom she is having an affair.

TRUE OR FALSE?

FALSE.

After supper, Danny Singer will stroll down to Murphy's Corner Grocery for a loaf of bread which Mavis forgot this afternoon (silly woman) and never come back.

TRUE OR FALSE?

FALSE.

After supper, Mavis Singer will ask Danny Singer for enough money for a one-way ticket back to Indian Mound.

TRUE OR FALSE?

FALSE.

After supper, the Singer family will live happily ever after.

THIS TOWN

A lot of the people in this town have come here from other places. There is always someone new in town, there is always someone just arriving (see POPULATION).

When you meet a new person in this town, the first questions are always the same.

"Where are you from?"

"How long have you been here?"

Some people will become friends on the basis of the answers to these and other questions.

Some people will say they were just passing through on their summer holidays and they had such a good time in this town that they just never left.

"That was two years ago last summer."

Because these people didn't come to this town on purpose, they never lose that sense of just passing through and so they are always talking about leaving.

Some of these people were on their way to the coast and now they are always talking about going there for the next long weekend. Some other people were on their way to California and now they always go there for their two-week vacation in the summer. They come back with furious suntans and color slides of the ocean.

In this town someone is always talking about leaving. Some of them do leave, but some of them don't. Most of those who do, come back in two months. Sometimes it is only when these people come back that the other people in this town notice they've been gone.

CLIMATE:

The standard saying in this town is: "If you don't like the weather, wait five minutes, it'll change." Living in this town means never knowing what to wear when you get up in the morning and then having to change your clothes four times a day anyway. This generates a lot of washing (see LAUNDROMAT). It is considered overly optimistic to go out without a jacket in July.

POPULATION:

There is room in this town for everyone. Someone is always arriving (coming to this town is easier than leaving it) but this town never gets any bigger and it never gets any smaller either.

Every other year they put a new number on the green sign on the highway. No one can ever remember what the last number was so no one ever knows if this town is gaining or losing ground.

Lorraine said, "We don't need to know anyway. Those signs are for tourists. They like to know these things" (see TOURISM).

PUBLIC HEALTH:

In this town someone always has or is just getting over a twenty-four hour bug. All such recurring afflictions are credited to the water, which is regularly infested by some kind of parasite that comes down off the mountains with the spring runoff.

All other afflictions are credited to the altitude and the thin mountain air.

Kevin said, "We are all suffering from chronic lack of oxygen."

This can be used to explain or excuse a number of things, including the milder forms of insanity and unhappiness.

Someone in this town always has a cold (see CLIMATE) or a virus.

ACCOMMODATION:

Most of the people in this town live in rented apartments or houses. These are very hard to come by. Everybody is always complaining that their rent is too high and so they are always moving to a smaller, cheaper place. Someone is always saying, "If you hear of anything coming up for rent, let me know." A lot of people, even families with children, keep renting because they are planning to leave in the spring (see GENERAL INFOR-MATION).

Some couples buy a lot in the new subdivision, which is the only part of town where the streets are paved. They like to build their own houses. This keeps them very busy. They are always working hard to make the mortgage payments which are usually higher than they bargained on. They are always planning patios, babies, and vegetable gardens.

The power of a nice new $100,000 house is never underestimated. Andy and Mary said, together, "Once we move in, we'll be so happy."

TOURISM:

In this town it is standard summer practice to go out for a walk on Sunday afternoon with or without the dog which you may or may not own (see PETS). You will be stopped on the average of five times and asked for directions.

Most of these tourists will want to know how to get back to the highway. Before beginning your walk, it is important to know how to get to: the golf course, the liquor store, a fast food place (there isn't one), a bathroom, a campground with hookups (it's full).

One Sunday a man in sunglasses in a big blue Buick said to Barb: "This is such a quaint little town. But what do all you people *do* here?"

ENTERTAINMENT:

In this town all roads lead to the bar. There might also be one road which leads to the pool hall. The pool hall is a recreational distraction. The bar, on the other hand, is a serious place where serious business occurs.

Connie said, "We were in the bar when Kevin told me he was leaving town and moving to the coast (see GENERAL INFORMATION). I was crying but nobody noticed and the beer kept coming. Pretty soon the whole table was covered with empty bottles. Leon kept lying them down on their sides and calling them dead soldiers. He was comforting me" (see LOVE).

In this town there is a dance once every two months. Most of the people in this town love to dance so everybody goes and nobody ever dances with the person they came with. This is important because of course everybody needs to feel free. The small town version of freedom means flirting with your best friend's husband or lover or both. It is likely that you will end up at the same table with three old lovers and one or two new lovers. Most of the people in this town are very civilized.

Most people in this town harbour a disproportionate fear of going home alone (see LOVE). This fear becomes especially prevalent on Saturday night.

Barb said, "I hate eating breakfast alone on Sunday. If a man is with me I make bacon and eggs and biscuits. Sometimes, if it's a special occasion or I think we might be in love, I make strawberry crepes. If I'm alone I have three cups of coffee and five or six cigarettes. I know that's unhealthy."

HOBBIES:

A lot of people in this town are always having dinner parties. In the summer they are always having barbecues.

Lorraine said, "I enjoy taking care of people. Everyone likes to eat, everyone tells me I'm a good cook. Maybe someday I'll become a chef. I'm happy when I'm watching someone eat."

Marshall, who is Lorraine's husband and also a realist, said, "You just like showing off. Life isn't a dinner party, Lorraine."

Lorraine and Marshall are always talking about leaving this town (see GENERAL INFORMATION) or getting a divorce (see MARRIAGE).

Most of the people in this town have, at one time or another taken up macramé, weaving, baking bread, gardening, running, and photography. Some people still do some or all of these things. Everybody owns a 35 mm camera with multiple interchangeable lenses. Most of the people in this town do not collect stamps or coins or salt and pepper shakers. Some people collect postcards or comic books.

PETS:

Everyone in this town loves animals. If you have a dog, it will be a German Shepherd, a Siberian Husky, or an Alaskan Malamute. If you don't have a dog, it will be because your landlady doesn't allow pets or because you are planning to leave town in the spring (see GENERAL INFORMATION) and you don't want to get tied down (see LOVE).

Some people have cats. Most people have more than one.

Barb said, "I'd be lost without them."

Someone in this town is always giving away kittens or puppies.

CHILDREN:

This town is very fertile. Someone is always pregnant. There is always someone wanting to buy your old baby carriage and your bassinette. Everybody believes in cloth diapers and breast-feeding and making your own baby food in the blender.

When the baby cries in a restaurant, the parents are embarrassed but they smile proudly.

Everybody is thankful for the Day Care Center which has just been established in town. The young mothers talk about how their children will grow up and be friends and go to school together.

LAUNDROMAT:

Almost none of the people in this town own a washer and dryer. Everybody goes to the laundromat, which is always full. Some of the washing machines are always breaking down. Most people go down the street to the bar while their clothes are drying (see ENTERTAINMENT).

Mary said, "If Indians are supposed to be dirty, my mother always said they were dirty, then why do they spend so much time in the laundromat?"

LOVE:

Some of the people in this town are congenitally reluctant to form attachments because they don't want to get tied down (see PETS). Most of these people have been hurt before in some other town and now they are afraid of meaningful relationships. These things, however, do not stop most people from devoting a lot of time to looking for love (see ENTERTAINMENT), even though they don't seem to know what they will do with it when they find it. They just don't like going home alone.

A lot of people think that having sex with a person is the only way to get to know them and to decide whether love is likely or not. It is educational to drive around this town early on a Saturday morning and see whose car is parked in front of (or behind, depending on the complexities of the situation) whose house.

Kevin said, "I call it the Lending Library."

When a couple breaks up, there is always some friend waiting to comfort the wounded party.

Leon said, "There's always some woman in the bar who needs to forget her troubles (see ENTERTAINMENT). I try not to miss these opportunities to be understanding."

When an unhealthy relationship finally ends, friends are relieved and they say, "I wanted to tell you before but I didn't."

Sex, if not love, is easy to come by in this town. Barb slept with six different men in a month and a half. This was immediately after her break-up with Bill, a carpenter she'd loved fiercely for two years and four months.

Barb's friends were all worried about her and they said:

"You'll get a reputation."

"You'll get a disease."

"You'll get hurt."

"You'll get pregnant."

"You'll get bitter and cynical."

"It's time to get serious."

MARRIAGE:

Most of the married people in this town are unhappy. Some of these unhappily married people are still giving dinner parties (see HOBBIES) and pretending to be happy.

At a dinner party at Lorraine and Marshall's house, Lorraine asked Mary, "How are you?"

Mary said, "I'm so happy it seems unnatural."

Lorraine said, "Have some more guacamole."

Some of these unhappily married people aren't pretending anymore and they are always talking to anybody who will listen about their marital problems and the merits of a trial separation.

At a dinner party at Andy and Mary's house, Mary asked Lorraine, "How are you?"

Lorraine said, "I'm miserable."

Marshall said, "I want a divorce."

Mary said, "Have some more guacamole."

There are wedding parties and sometimes there are divorce parties. Everybody always gets drunk at parties.

At wedding parties, some of the guests are talking about when their divorce date is coming up. At one wedding party, the bride said, "If we get divorced, I won't ask for a thing." Hugging her, the groom said, "That's my girl."

At divorce parties, some people are always talking about how important it is to stay friends.

DEATH:

Susan said, "When I was a child one day my father was in the basement trying to kill himself. Of course I was too young to understand how someone I loved could be that upset. After I unloaded the gun, I called the doctor. After the doctor left, my father went upstairs to his bedroom and rested. For five years my father didn't speak to me. After five years, I asked my mother to tell me why. She said it was because he thought that I thought he was crazy."

Ed said, "Well, of course he was crazy."

Three years ago, Ed tried to kill himself with pills, not a gun. In this town one death has nothing to do with another.

SHE WANTS TO TELL ME

YOU'RE SITTING THERE like a bouquet of flowers, pastel, perfumed and conspicuous. You want to tell me your whole life story. You also want another drink. How can I refuse you either? How can I refuse you anything?

You say, "Your geraniums are lovely."

It's that special single hour on a late summer's evening when the light has gone all sentimental, the birds are singing dementedly, and way out in suburbia, some beautiful virgin boy is mowing his mother's lawn, flexing his thighs, and dreaming he's the singer in a rock and roll band.

"I've never had much luck with flowers myself," you tell me. "I find it easier just to let some man buy them for me."

Here our downtown birds are ratty old pigeons, circling aimlessly, preening and cooing at nothing. Our downtown boys in their black leather jackets are always playing video games, flexing their fingers, hooked, and I can't imagine what they might be dreaming. Most of them will survive.

"They always die on me."

You sniff the breeze, which is supposed to smell like berries or white sand, but in this neighborhood is mostly exhaust. You massage it into your bare arms anyway, stretching your legs, kicking off your shoes (which are perfect) and settling in. The soles of your feet are dirty and smooth, like a child's.

"The flowers, I mean."

Our ice cubes are melting. I'll go in and get some more. I wish I had an ice bucket, a silver one. You do. You must.

"Expensive feet, I've always had expensive feet. I can only

149

wear Italian shoes. It gets to be like a curse. I had to search the whole city to find such marvellous shoes."

And here I sit, me with my plain old peasant feet, domestic feet propped up on a flower pot, swelling and smelling in the heat.

Get more wine. Also domestic. But you are, I imagine, too well-bred to notice.

"It hardly smells like summer anymore," you observe. "The nights are getting cooler, longer. Where does the time go? It seems to pass so slowly but always carries on, and then in the end, it's nothing but gone. This wine is delicious."

You think you're in Italy, Paris, on the Riviera or the Virgin Islands, anywhere but here, examining your fingernails, tucking your hair behind one ear, pulling up your lacy white skirt to catch the last of the sun. You think that I'm just like you — which is flattering but nerve-wracking. I'd hate like hell to disillusion you.

"In the beginning I just loved this building. Being up in the air like this, I thought I was on top of the world."

The balconies on either side, above and below us, are like blinkers. They are cluttered with various junky but revealing accumulations: gas barbecues, an exercise bike, water skis, a baby carriage, underwear and pantyhose draped over the side, red geraniums and a sleeping bag — these last being mine. I like to sleep out here when it's hot. The bugs don't bother me much.

"But sometimes now I feel like a little girl up in the attic playing dress-up, clomping around in my mother's high-heels."

There's a siren in the street. I can almost hear the crowd converging. But we're up high enough here to be immune. At least we like to think so.

"All dressed up and no place to go."

Directly across is another high-rise, higher, with offices inside — doctors, lawyers, psychiatrists, I suppose. The windows are all copper-colored, like those expensive pots and pans you always see hanging around magazine kitchens.

"Other times I get to thinking about all those people below

me, layers and layers of them, doing whatever it is that normal people do — watching TV, making popcorn or love, putting their babies to bed. They don't know that I'm walking around on their heads. They don't care. But sometimes," you tell me, "sometimes, I can feel their hard little skulls under my bare feet like pebbles."

You were out on your balcony, right next door, when I came out here onto mine. Leaning against the railing, you were shielding your eyes with one hand and peering up at the sky. No, more like into it, deeply. Watching for something, a flock of fabulous birds, an alien invasion by air, or maybe a sign from God. Your balcony is empty, tells me nothing.

"Hunter says I'm starting to sound crazy again. He says, 'Marguerite, you're losing it.' But maybe I'm just fooling around."

Finally you turned toward me and, ordinarily enough, waved across. I beckoned you over with my frosted glass, wanting to share the wine so I could dispense with feeling guilty about drinking alone.

"I met Hunter in a tavern in Toronto. He was there with his buddies for a beer after work, watching the strippers and pumping the pinball machine full of quarters. I have no idea now what I was doing there. Hiding. Finding him in a dump like that made him seem more real than the rest. I still thought falling in love was an acceptable practice. For a few months anyway, I took Hunter to be an ordinary man, normal, decent and dependable. Which was what I thought I wanted. That was then."

Next to you, Marguerite, Hunter is ordinary (lots of men these days wear earrings — I know that), so ordinary that he could be almost anything to you: lover, husband, best friend, second cousin twice-removed. It's hard to tell. He's too dark to be your brother. There is about the two of you none of that aggressive self-insistent happiness which marks newlyweds and people who are together when they shouldn't be.

"We came here by accident, more of an experiment than a

decision, the transplant of something vital into something else."

I was glad when you moved in. That apartment had been vacant for months and I'd pretty well given up on the people on the other side. They're an old foreign couple with a pack of little rat dogs over-running their apartment. Their grown-up children come over on Sundays with casseroles, pies and flowers done up like wreaths — as if they've already died and gone to heaven. Maybe they think they have.

"I never dream about him anymore. Mostly now I dream about babies, having them, losing them, buying them. I also dream about trains, catching them, missing them. Sometimes they're coming right into the bedroom. If you dream about a dead cat, what do you think that means?" you ask me. "Hunter holds me when I wake up crying but it doesn't help anymore."

I've been listening to the sounds from your apartment but all I get is the usual: vacuum cleaner, sometimes rock and roll records turned up too loud, the bed banging against the wall, the occasional argument in the middle of the night but I can never make out the words and there are no dishes breaking.

"You know what I mean."

Somewhere over the years, I have become the kind of woman other people feel compelled to confide in. Time and again I've kept my big mouth shut on all sorts of serpents and secrets, justifying their faith in me.

"You're so easy to talk to."

But other times too, I've come home from an evening with friends, half-drunk, tender and sobbing with the sheer weight of knowing so many things about so many people. They give me too much credit, they forget that I'm a person, not just a receptacle. I can spill things too. The beans. My guts. The wine. I can be dangerous too, not always just vicarious.

"My first husband's name was Frederick."

I've always hated that name. Makes me think of a beagle with slippers in its mouth.

"We met on a Mexican beach where we had both gone to recuperate — from different things, of course. I was just out of the hospital and he was just out of a miserable marriage in Vancouver. He'd lived there all his life, brilliant and crazy, always wanting to dive off a high-rise into the sea. I wanted to meet a genius. I wanted to meet a maniac. Frederick was the man of my dreams. In that warm water we were like swordfish, supple and salty and tasty. We were young. Six months later we flew back to Mexico and were married on that very same beach. My bridal bouquet burned up in the sun. More wine please."

We're well into our second bottle now. It's a good thing I keep a supply in. You just never know when you'll need another drink.

Now that I've got you here, I don't want to think of you jumping up and running away.

"Back home, marriage was nothing like Mexico or swimming, nothing at all. I told him what I wanted but he wasn't listening, or maybe he was down by the sea."

You're talking in code and assuming, in the way of unhappy young women, that I know much more or much less than I do. You're right either way.

"I want them to know I'm a person, not just a place."

I'm wanting to believe everything you're telling me. I'm willing to listen to anything. Nothing about you can surprise me now.

"I nearly drowned once when I was a child, but I got over it. I'm a superb swimmer now, so they tell me."

There is no way of knowing if what you tell me is true. But that, I suppose, can be said of most people. The truth, like old wooden houses in the winter, is always shifting, cracking, settling back down in some other season, some other place. Nobody wants to admit that truth, like time, can never stand still. It is always a becoming, always a changing, always a staying-the-same.

"I was already sick by that time and was supposed to stay in bed all day. I was happier then than I've ever been since. I always kept the curtains closed. One wall was filled with floor-to-ceiling bookshelves. I read with a flashlight so I didn't have to open the drapes. The other wall was covered with dolls and stuffed animals, hung from little hooks by little strings around their little necks. Their bulging faces only frightened me when I was delirious from the drugs or the pain. The rest of the time they were quite friendly. But I still can't sleep if there's any part of me, even one toe, hanging off the edge of the bed."

I can't sleep in the bed at all. In the summer I sleep out here. In the winter I sleep on the couch. Nobody knows this about me. I sleep alone.

"There was one doctor who said there was nothing wrong with me. He said it was all in my head."

You know what they say: Two heads are better than one.

"We got rid of him."

It was all in his head.

"Everything I wanted came to me before I even had to ask for it. Silent nurses relayed tray after tray up the stairs. They would slide into my room, sighing and patting my hair, spoon-feeding me sometimes, bringing me whatever I cried for: icing sugar, jelly beans, lemonade, pink mints."

More wine.

"My tutors were all handsome young men who seemed to be hiding from something. My favorite was the one who taught me how to play the banjo and five-card stud. About everything else, he couldn't care less."

Me neither.

"I just naturally assumed this was how all little girls were treated. And if they weren't, they should be. I thought everyone was just like me. Or wanted to be."

Some things never change.

"Once I saw a man beating a little dog in the gutter with a baseball bat. When I tried to stop him, he swung at me too.

This was either in Mexico or Toronto, I forget which. This was later."

It's as if you're wrapped in something. Valium or some vague aura, mysterious but convincing. The sunset, the wine, your slack voice, all are equally potent, and I am captured by the puzzle, the pieces you offer me, one at a time, like grapes. Everything is going wine-colored around me, especially your hair, with the sun going down all through it.

"My father was a diplomat, whatever that means. It was never really explained to me and I never thought to ask. It was enough to know that he was someone important, always dressed in a three-piece suit, talking on the telephone, bringing home presents, buying black cars, always going away again."

My father was an alcoholic, whatever that means.

"Most of the time he ignored me, which was comforting."
, *Comforting enough.*

"He's retired now, my old man, still handsome and lolling around exclusive hotels, sending me postcards that I stick on the bathroom wall. He never interested me much anyway."

I picture the old man lounging in a hot tub, sucking on crab legs, white grapes, the succulent oiled shoulder of some ripe debutante. He drinks dry martinis all day long. He beckons for a pen, dashes off something slightly witty, slumps back into the water, his fatherly impulses stifled or satisfied for now. Having a wonderful time. Glad you're not here. You never interested him much anyway.

"My mother's funeral was a discreetly grand affair. Nobody asked the uncomfortable questions and only her old black maid, Maisie, was primitive or generous enough to cry. There were thousands of flowers, white lilies mostly, her favorite, like snowbanks on the altar. I wore the most gorgeous blue silk, raw silk — everyone loved it."

The more you drink, the more your accent goes southern. Imagining you in front of a white pillared mansion becomes irresistible. In ten starched crinolines, you're waving and weeping till your eyes are like bruised peaches and the tops of your breasts swell and pulse. Two blue peacocks, dazzling and heartless, strut stiffly around you. An old yellow dog lies on the lawn, sleeping or dead. Your man is going off to war (Civil) and we all know he'll never come back. Sad, so sad, this scene is so sad it should be on the cover of a romance novel. Somewhere in it there are also magnolia blossoms, in your hair or scattered around your feet.

Oh shit. Frankly Scarlett, I don't give a damn.

"My mother had no influence on me, none at all."

This cannot, is not, will never be true.

"Once I thought she never really wanted me."

Once I thought I could see the future but it was only a coincidence.

"But then she left me a fortune."

Fortunes. I collect them, the kind that come in cookies: You will have good luck and overcome many hardships. For better luck you have to wait till autumn. You will receive a gift from a friend. Good news will come to you from far away.

I figure if I keep them long enough, they're bound to come true.

"When I was a little girl, I wanted to be a fortune teller."

And what are you now? Don't you dare start reading my mind.

"My second husband, Max, was killed six months after the wedding. It was his own damn fault. That was when I decided I would never get married again. There's nothing sure in this world."

I'll drink to that.

"Hit by a bus."

The nerve of some people.

"Just that morning, we'd bought tickets to Spain. I went by myself but it wasn't the same. I'd forgotten about the bulls."

I'm afraid to imagine the sound.

"Once I saw a chicken with its head cut off running by the side of the road. That was in Spain too."

Once I chopped a chicken's head off with an axe. The axe was dull and it took a long time. That was on the farm. Then we made soup for supper.

"The thing about travelling is you're always thinking that the next restaurant, hotel room, city or country will be the perfect one, the one thing you've been searching for all your little life. I could have been a gypsy if I'd wanted to."

Even your purse is like a suitcase, lumpy with eccentric items, I imagine — a hammer, a box of sugar cubes, and a syringe.

"In a hotel room in Paris, I found a photo album stashed behind the bed. Everyone in it looked happy and French, black and white. There were all combinations, young and old, men and women, with statues, horses, dogs, hugging each other. Everywhere there were trees, flowers, windows, rocking chairs, lace. There was a whole series of women clowning in white face for Hallowe'en or a play, doing mime in the street. Every little thing looked French. This is my favorite."

In the photograph you hand me, four young women are lounging around a fountain with flowerbeds. They're dressed in loose long skirts and sandals, resting their heads and hands on each other, lovingly. They're carrying things, paper bags, purses, a sweater. They're going somewhere, shopping, home, or out of the country. They look quite beautiful and intense, yes, very French. If they could talk, I wouldn't know what they were saying.

Why are you carrying these handsome anonymous women around in your purse as if they were good old friends?

"I want to be just like them. I want to be in the picture."

What you tell me is like marbles, those clear glass ones, green that you can see through if you hold one up to your eyeball. Marbles, the big ones, hard and flawless, no avenue in. They hit off each other in the dirt, spin away in tangents, out of reach altogether.

"When we moved into this place, I found a hundred dollar bill behind the stove."

What are you doing always looking behind things, beds and stoves, looking for other people's treasures or castoffs, finding them too? I found a diamond ring once but I sold it.

"I thought it was a lucky omen."

I thought you were perfect.

"Sometimes, just to cheer myself up, I use some of the money to send myself flowers. And then I pretend I don't know who they're from."

I thought you were going to teach me something, maybe how to swim.

"All I want to do is sleep."

You're no longer emotionally charming.

"The worst thing about being in jail that time was having to phone home and explain why I wouldn't be there for Christmas."

You're too young to know so much.

"I've never liked Christmas much anyway."

Too bad.

"I thought it would be different."

It is.

"Everything, I mean."

Are we drunk yet?

"It wasn't my fault."

I'm just feeling bitchy.

"You'll see what I mean when I tell you."

I'll try.

"All my lies are white ones."

There he is now, just in time, Hunter on the next balcony, waving "Hello" and "Come home" in one simple gesture. He's so graceful for a man. You gulp down your wine, gather up your purse, your perfect shoes, rush off barefoot and unsteady. Why are we looking so guilty? He's so powerful for a man.

You're off to your apartment which, I imagine, is laid out just like mine and furnished finely but starkly. Vivid white walls, old wicker painted black, pink vases and pillows scattered around strategically. These are called accents. No plants — they would die. No dirt — of course not. There may be a red stain somewhere on the white rug but it could be anything. It could have been there when you moved in.

158

There is also an aquarium, full of flowers instead of fish.

You're off now to perform unimaginable acts: making filet mignon, juicy and rare; overseas phone calls; love.

I'm just going to sit here awhile and finish my wine. As soon as I lie down in the dark, I'll be trying not to listen. You're not quite a stranger anymore, an intimate one if you are. I know too much now to invent you.

I want to tell you my whole life story.

LIFE SENTENCES

THEY'VE KNOWN EACH OTHER, this woman, this man, ever since they were kids, healthy, wealthy and (   ). For all their young lives, they lived in identical ranch-style homes side by side on West (   ) Avenue. Both their fathers were important energetic men in the (   ) Company downtown and their mothers were (   ) housewives, lazy and slim.

They were both only children, growing up smoothly with a strong sense of their own (   ) power. Everywhere they looked there was money or signs of it. Money was not something they ever had to (   ) about. They lived comfortable lucky lives, exclusive (   ) lives. They knew nothing of pain or suffering, danger or (   ). Such things did not seem (   ) or possible.

As adults, they share (   ) memories of lavish turkey dinners, shiny bicycles, picnics at the cottage on Lake (   ), and washing the Cadillacs with their dads on Saturday afternoon in the sunshine. Their moms are sitting in one kitchen or the other, slopping up brandy until they come outside angry and squinting and (   ), refusing to cook. These kids don't care, they don't know any (   ).

They were innocent together, this girl, this boy. They have no sense now of having met; they might as well have been (   ), that's how close they were.

One day in high school the young woman looked (   ) at the young man and saw that he was remarkable. She knew then that she wanted to spend the rest of her (   ) with him and only him. There was no reason to think that she wouldn't.

She'd always got what she (   ) before.

They did everything together in those halcyon days and their parents thought they were (   ) and cute. They went to movies, dances and football parties, holding (   ), smiling and kissing in corners. They made (   ) love in the back seat of the car the young man's parents bought him for his (   ) birthday. The young woman loved it when he put his (   ) in her (   ). She was filling up her hope chest with crystal, fine linen and (   ). She just naturally assumed that the young man (   ) her as much as she (   ) him. He certainly (   ) as if he did.

Of course their parents all approved. Their fathers were talking about retiring early and buying a condo in (   ), which was all the rage at the time. Their mothers were still drunk half the time and now these two kids understood that such behaviour was (   ) and likely to drive them to the same psychiatrist in later years.

After high school, the young man smashed up his car and walked away without a (   ) to some fancy college in (   ). The young woman stayed behind and sold novels in a bookstore while she (   ) for him to come home. Her rich parents said this lousy job was (   ) for her.

They wrote letters back and forth, this young woman, this young man, long letters, (   ) letters, unsatisfying letters. It was only after the young man came home for Christmas the second year with a (   ) gypsy girl that the young woman realized he might not (   ) her after all. Some men when you (   ) them, you know that somehow, slowly, they're going to defeat you. She was (   ) but he wasn't paying attention anymore. So she pretended to be (   ) and succeeded. He was (   ) fooled.

The man and the gypsy were married the next summer in his parents' backyard. The woman was invited of course and had to go just to show him she wasn't (   ).

But the young woman still (   ) the young man. She got fat,

fat, fatter, sad, sad, sadder, and her broken heart was driving her ( ). So her worried parents sent her away to Europe for a little ( ). She came home much thinner and much ( ). She hated the young man now, which was much easier than ( ) him.

In a few years, the young woman, who was no longer feeling young, married a doctor who ( ) her desperately and bought her a mansion filled with wonderful things right on ( ) Street, the best part of town. Her parents didn't really like this doctor but they figured he was better than ( ). So did the woman. She didn't really ( ) this doctor but figured she'd learn to in time. The young man was ( ) and didn't make it to the wedding. He sent along a Cuisinart instead. The young woman's parents thought that was the end of that. Not likely, not by a ( ) shot.

Shortly afterwards, the young man's father ( ) himself tragically in the head, his mother promptly ( ) herself to death, and the young man inherited everything, through no ( ) of his own. He had so much money then, he would never have to work again. It was all very ( ).

As it turned out, the mansion he bought for his gypsy wife happened to be on the same street as the mansion of the woman and her doctor husband. He said it was an accident, purely ( ). By now he had a set of gypsy twins and another ( ) on the way. He was always buying new Cadillacs and smashing them up, a ridiculous habit that nobody ( ) seriously. He was just like a cat with ( ) lives, extended lives, flaunting them. The woman had become a writer of ( ) poetry and no longer found it necessary to ( ) the man. She was writing about other things now anyway. Absence makes the ( ) grow ( ). They were both getting older and ( ), in spite of themselves.

So they decided to become friends again, ( ) at first and then ( ). Pretty soon, it was as though they'd never been ( ).

The man teaches the doctor how to ( ) and, in return, the doctor teaches the man how to ( ). They have many things in ( ), the two men discover. They love the same restaurants, the same sports, the same ( ). After a while, they even begin to ( ) alike.

Sometimes the woman babysits the gypsy twins and the new baby, who is a ( ). She has never liked kids but it seems the ( ) she can do for that ( ) woman. She and the gypsy go shopping together, drink ( ), laugh about ( ) and talk about ( ). Everyone thinks the two women are ( ) friends and in a way they are too.

The woman and the man are glad to be ( ) again after all that's happened. They tell each other ( ) and they kiss in corners on New Year's Eve. Once or twice the doctor accuses the woman of having an ( ) with the man but of course that isn't strictly true. Still though, he says she just wants to have her ( ) and eat it too.

One day at lunch the man confessed to the woman that his marriage was ( ). The woman was hardly surprised — indeed, this seemed in retrospect to be exactly what she'd ( ) all along. The gypsy said the man was a ( ). The man said the gypsy was a ( ). They would never be ( ) again so there was no use trying. It was nobody's fault.

Not long afterwards, the doctor announced he was in ( ) with the gypsy. Everybody was surprised but there was ( ) to be done about it now. The doctor said the woman had never really ( ) him. The woman said that was true, ( ) but true. There was no one to blame. They were all very civilized people, unlucky maybe, but ( ).

After the divorces, which were unfriendly but ( ), the man and the woman stuck together. It was the ( ) thing to do. They ( ) each other.

The woman soon sold her mansion and moved all her furniture down the street. The gypsy's furniture was ( )

anyway, so they sold it. The woman wanted to burn it but the man said she was being (   ).

By this time, the woman's parents had moved down south to the dream condo in (   ) and she was glad she no longer had to face them. Her psychiatrist had helped her understand that she would never be able to (   ) them, no matter what she did. It was the curse of only children that their parents were never (   ), never satisfied.

This same psychiatrist had also helped the man realize he would never be happy either and his trouble with those Cadillacs was a (   ) wish. They were working on their problems (   ), this woman, this man, and it was no wonder they had so many, considering the way their monstrous mothers had (   ) them.

The man and the woman had all the same friends as before and nobody seemed to (   ) that the doctor and the gypsy had disappeared. It was as though those other two had never been much (   ) anyway. There was no need to get married now: once bitten, twice (   ). Besides, they were too old to have (   ) now anyway — it was too late for some things, lots of things, (   ) things.

Their lives, twin lives, discolored, go on and on and always (   ). They still like to (   ) and (   ) and (   ). They still love the same (   ), the same (   ) and the same (   ). The man is still buying Cadillacs, and the woman is still writing poetry. She knows that they're supposed to be (   ) at last. What more could they (   ) for? But her poems are all about (   ) and the man just wrecked another one.

Today the man is out in the driveway washing the Cadillac. The woman is thinking that if she has to watch him do this one more time she will (   ), just (   ). She's in the kitchen drinking (   ) and getting meaner and (   ) by the minute. She knows this drinking is a (   ) habit. She knows she's just like her (   ). How depressing, how (   ), how true.

It seems that there are only two more things she can do in

her life: stay with this man till ( ) freezes over or ( ) him. He'd be better off ( ) anyway.

Either way, she knows she will never be free of him. This man does not ( ) her, she knows that now, she's sure he never did, she's sure he never will. He knows her too well, all too ( ). Familiarity breeds ( ). She keeps wishing he'd drive the new Cadillac over a cliff and be ( ) with it. She can just see the flames, she can just hear the ( ), she can almost taste the gallons of ( ). The one thing she has never been in her life is alone.

She goes through all the ways she could do it, one by one. The possibilities are ( ). She thinks that ( ) would be best — bloodless, tidy and ( ). No one will ever know. She's sure she'll get away with it — she's led a charmed life. No one will even ( ) her. She is above suspicion, though not above ( ).

The clouds are ( ), the ill wind is ( ), it looks like it's going to ( ).

Life, it seems from this vantage point, tends, intends, to go on for a very long time. There is no one to blame, no one to thank, no one but ( ).

WAITING

After a time even the sound of the television stopped. Dory couldn't tell how long she had lain awake listening to it. The voices of women had come to her for hours perhaps, woman voices with no words, soft and sudden, as if they were talking in their sleep. Soon Dory stopped listening for them and listened instead for those other voices, deeper voices.

Man voices. Making little waves that roll right through my belly, not my ears. Like water waves. Just like when my dad sat me down in the sand at the beach. Just like that time and the waves came up over my belly.

Just before the silence came, Dory heard familiar music coming through the bedroom wall and through the woollen blankets tucked up tight around her ears. Dory held her breath, straining and hoping to hear. She caught and remembered the song just in patches. It made her think of plywood and big blackboards and chalk. All of these things became tangled up in the song.

What song? Throats singing fast, yes, too fast, and slowed down then by some other throat. Grown-up throat wearing a wool suit and nylons and green high-heels. That throat with no first name. Only "Miss" and last name "Burns." Miss Burns singing this same song and she leads the room by its throat through the notes with her pointer. Fingers made of chalk and chalk on her cheeks too. Cheeks that move up and down and sing this song. Calls it "anthem."

The song was the signal for another day to begin. And once it had been sung, she could sit down at her plywood desk and wait to be told to open her books for the day. And Miss Burns, standing up at the blackboard, would always call her "Doria" and she would sit up even straighter then, trying to make the full name fit. But none of this could happen until the song had been sung. Until it had been sung by everyone all the way through to the end, time and the day could not begin to pass. But now Dory could not sing: the song had lost its words somewhere and Miss Burns wasn't there to rescue her. Without Miss Burns' throat to push the music into line, there could be no song.

The silence came with a click. Dory could picture that girl out there in the living room turning off the song before it could end. And now time could not pass. That girl out there turned off the music, not wanting the evening ever to end. That girl who came over only when Dory's parents were going out for the evening.

"Estelle" they call her. Or "the babysitter." She means they've got to go. Her face at the front door makes them leave. Why leave? House too small maybe. Not room enough for all of us here and so then they leave.

You're just being silly.

I know.

The screen door had closed tight and fast on their backs when they left early that night. Dory's mother was still saying goodbye when it slapped shut.

Now another sound came into Dory's room. Another sound somehow familiar, everything from out there seemed to sound familiar from inside her room. This sound was soft and shuffling. Like wool and slippers.

Yes, that girl has feet with slippers on. Wool with pink puffballs stuck to the tops of her toes. Good for walking on floors in the winter.

Dory rolled over in her bed and the covers rolled with her.

The sheets twisted up around her legs, close and tight like drying skin. She looked up through the darkness to the ceiling and discovered a new game to play with the porcelain light globe. Looking straight at the spot where she knew it hung, she could see nothing. But if she turned her head and let her eyes sidle slowly up to the spot . . . there it was. At least it was there until, in her slow sidling, she was finally looking straight at the spot again. And then the white globe was gone. The game kept Dory amused for some time. But then came the sound of the back door opening and closing.

The door is locked. No one home. No one? That girl is gone now. And only I am home.

In her bedroom with the door shut, Dory could not know that the back door had been shut and then locked from the inside. She could not know that Estelle was stretched out on the sofa, already falling asleep. Dory's parents would not be home until the next day. They had gone to spend the night at a neighbor's camp. Dory was left at home because there would be snowmobiling ("Too dangerous," her father had said) and then liquor and lots of ribald jokes ("Hardly the thing for little girls," her mother had said).

Dory lay awake now waiting for their home-coming sound, for the sound of their car outside in the street. When it came, the sound would spread itself out flat in the street like new snow.

Headlights grazed the bedroom ceiling, laser beams of light. And then the same darkness drew back deeper into the room. Dory undid her legs from the bedsheets, unravelled her flannelette nightgown from where it had spun itself around her shoulders.

The house was quiet. To Dory, the silence simply proved that she was alone. Her feet felt for the floor.

Floor is wet? No, just cold. So cold it sticks to my skin. Like when my tongue got stuck to the car door handle. Cars went by and I cried there stuck. And my dad laughed while he undid me.

And then?

Blood and my mother made me drink warm milk. Silly girl, she said. And I felt silly too. I cried and she smiled. So silly.

Dory crouched down in front of the bedroom window. Her fingers gripped the wooden sill with little peanut knuckles. The sound of the car outside continued. She could see it now. But it wasn't their car. This one was too small, kneeling down there beside the snowbanks and the garbage can. Theirs was bigger and blacker.

The door of the car opened and a girl climbed out, nursing her purse close against the cold. She walked away from the car without looking back, as if it were no longer there, as if she no longer thought at all of the one she was leaving behind.

Leaving? Must leave. Not room enough for everybody in that so little car. She doesn't care. People leaving never care, do they? No, and the ones who're left, they don't care either. Neither do I. Everybody smiles through goodbye. Smiles? Yes, because they'll come back. They? That girl, Mom, Dad, family, me. We all smile.

Cold now, like the tile, Dory's feet slid across the floor as she groped her way back to the bed. She heard the car drive away.

After a time, Dory stopped listening for them. And listened instead to her breath and to another breath which seemed to come from the back side of the door. It was, she decided, the breath of the house.

And who will sing my house to sleep? Not me. No one. It will just sit and wait. Maybe it can't ever sleep. Never? No, and I won't again either.

Dory was not afraid. She had not been alone often enough to know that there might be a reason to be afraid. Her parents did not come home.

Why not? I don't know. Forgot maybe? Well, I won't forget. Won't go to sleep either. Keep my eyes open. Open? Yes, but just let me close them for a minute. Hurt from looking at nothing for so long. Nothing? Well . . . at the dark then. And that's nothing.

Just let me close them for one more minute. One more little minute. Just one more . . .

Dory could not have known when she fell asleep.

Afterwards, she wouldn't even know for sure whether she had or not.

TWO: CAROLINE

Caroline resisted the impulse to turn on the television set. She sat in an armchair lodged in one corner of the room. The throw cover had slid down the high back and lay in a bunch at the small of her back. Annoyed, she leaned forward. A spring bounced up hard beneath her.

Rearranging herself to avoid both the throw and the spring, Caroline stroked the uncovered arm of the chair.

Stroking: such a comfortable motion. Stroking everything back to passivity. Passive like passion. From the same word. And we're in love so passively, letting its moments enfold us, and we are passionate together. But passive apart. When apart? Now. Alone for a time and in love. How long in love? Forget now when it all began. Like Christmas Eve that way. On Christmas Eve there is no past. Only future. And waiting for the morning. Waiting now for Matthew to come home. Will come. Before the morning. Long before.

A freight train shunted cars on the track which ran parallel to the house. Somewhere in the kitchen a dish rattled and the metal kettle shuddered on the stove.

My ears and the room fill up . . . with? Sound in simple waves. Like the ones that get caught up in a seashell. Remember that day on the beach and I found a conch when the tide went away. Listening to the sea inside it: I felt just like this. Will tell Matthew when he gets home. But no. Remember what he said about the conch: not the sea, silly girl; logical explanation for this common phenomenon. And everyone knows that science has taken the sea out of seashells. Silly girl.

A novel lay open on the table close to her chair. Caroline picked it up. She read one more page, skimming. The floor was vibrating slightly under her toes.

Vibrating. Like waves in the wind. No, not waves again. Just a simple freight train. Or maybe just the rhythm of these written, rewritten words. Catches at my veins. Beating them back into shape. Hammer on tin. I wish I'd been the one who wrote these or some other words. Lots of words all laid out in lines. Laid out on pages spread out flat on Matthew's lap. He could take my words with him then. When he couldn't take me. There would be no forgetting then. And he does forget me, yes, when I'm not there. A door closes on my face and he is walking away and forgetting. Fast. Like now.

Caroline put the book down in her lap and stretched her arms out long before her. The deep pull of her muscles made her yawn.

The hours spun away on the clock-face. Caroline's confidence dipped away at random intervals. And anxiety filled up the space.

What if . . . an accident? Out there somewhere away from me, forgetting me and the car steers itself off the road. Into the ditch in silence. Why silence? Shouldn't there be metal ripping and white bones bruising, burning black? No. I'm not there. No sound with no ears to hear. No sound? Well, maybe just sad singing. From the sky or maybe from this mouth, my mouth, here.

She hummed a tune out into the room. But her lips were dry and sometimes the song sucked in the silence instead of displacing it. She hummed her way through every nursery rhyme she knew, tying the notes up in ribbons with her cigarette tongue. The ashtray balanced on the arm of the chair was bulging with butts. Caroline frowned at it.

Like squirrels. With wrinkled brown tails and acorn cheeks fat with waiting for winter that day. Walking that day together through the bushes and trees way out there. Past the city limits somewhere. And Matthew wondered when the squirrels gathered up those nuts and when the trees sprouted all those leaves. We never saw them do it. Only talked. Talking our way around so many trees — some were dead — and he told me things. All those forest things he'd read about in school.

Caroline stood up and crossed the room to the window. Her hair hung down her back in two thick braids. No one thought this unusual for a woman her age anymore. All her friends kept their hair short and curly but they'd grown accustomed to her braids. She pushed open the drapes which had become warped and slightly discolored with this constant habit of hers. Even when the drapes were closed now, an uneven oval of the outside showed through.

She watched the street and tried to pretend she wasn't alone.

And when I turn my back to the window again he will be there. In the chair, reading the book, the one with the blue binding. The one I've been reading. My book for now. Can share the same words anyway. And smoking too. He will be smoking like I was. And I'll see the smoke poking holes in his hair and I'll laugh when it gets in the way of words. The smoke seduces me and the words do too.

Caroline turned from the window. Of course the chair was still empty. And the only smoke in the room was not curling up through the air but lying in layers instead, stale and thin and dry.

He'll come home when he's done what he's got to do. Has to see some people first. Faces, just faces, no names. His friends, not mine. Work faces, the ones he spends the day with. Saves the nights for me. When we are together, they're left alone. But before that can happen, some things must be done.

Matthew buys them drinks and then he drinks some too. With them. Cheers. Being friendly. What does that mean to him? Buying drinks and food. Rare sirloin steak and mushrooms and salad. No sour cream on my baked potato, just butter, thanks. Smells good. Tastes better.

He buys more food when somebody new joins the group. He is somewhere out there in a room full of little round tables and three-legged chairs and music and drinks full of ice cubes and hot food and faces and fresh smoke and walls without windows and legs arms hands teeth.

Caroline looked out the window again, watching the world through well-polished glass. The red brick bungalow directly across the street was brightly lit and six cars were parked against the curb in front. Their roofs were littered with yellow wet leaves that dripped steadily down from the birches on the boulevard. She pictured a cluster of shiny-skinned people laughing into those bright little rooms.

This time the spring did not jump when Caroline fit herself back into the armchair. She leaned her head up against its high back.

It's early yet. It's early yet.

She chanted the lie to herself in a monotone, believing that this combination of words would work magic, would work her a spell that would make it all true.

She thought that when Matthew did arrive, she would cry, just at first, just when he came in the door.

But not now. My tears are no use when there's no one here to catch them. Catch them? Yes, with his fingers imported fresh from the world. Fingers factory-sealed in new leather gloves, vacuum-packed.

Just in case she fell asleep before he arrived, Caroline left the back door unlocked. He might have forgotten his key.

And yes he will come. And open the door and carry his love for me inside with him. A carefully obedient love. Kept on a leash, three paces back, with a choke chain. It will heel on command. And it even plays dead.

She leaned back further and deeper into the chair. The buttons on the back felt round and large, protruding like somebody's eyes.

Matthew did not come home. Caroline let herself fall asleep and she missed the sun just starting to rise.

173

It was a Friday sometime in March. Or it might have been Thursday and it might have been in April. Hannah reached for the little cardboard calendar — Courtesy of Your Friendly Neighborhood Bank: We Care About Our Customers — on the chest beside the bed.

Surprise. Wrong again. All wrong. It's a Monday in May. Which means? Nothing in particular. Or it might mean warm rain and children slopping through puddles in plastic yellow rainboots. Making waves in the oil-skinned water. Waves and they shine. Means there should be sun. But no, it's night now. Means darkness moist like breath.

Hannah strained to put the calendar back in place on the night table and almost missed it in the dark. The flesh of her upper arm hung like raw bread dough. She thought about her arm, her body.

Belongs to this house, this room, these covers too. Something's coming soon to catch it up and go. What something? Morning maybe . . . or? You know. No, tell me. But you already know. Maybe, but I want to hear you say the word. All right then: death.

Oh.

With the sound of an electric typewriter driven too long, drops of rain broke against the metal awning outside her bedroom window. It was a familiar sound and Hannah was quite calm with the waiting.

Waiting here for the end. It will come. Of course. No more illusions. Old women all die, always. I'm not afraid. Not eager either. Just waiting.

Hannah was well-prepared. Her will was made, her estate was in order, the house was neat and uncommonly clean. She'd spent all afternoon washing and waxing and dusting just to be ready for this company that she knew would come. Both the front and back doors were unlocked.

Today will be the day. Because it's a Monday in May and there's no better time than right now. Today is the very last day. I have decided. I'm ready.

She waited without wondering what it would be like to die. Long ago she'd realized that it wouldn't be like anything. It would just be. There was no sense then in wondering about death, let alone worrying about it, as so many of her younger friends had. Most of them were dead now anyway.

She began plotting her meals for the next day. This was a ritual, the only foolproof way to find sleep. Breakfast came first of course. She prided herself on always following the natural order of things.

For breakfast then? Porridge. Just the thought makes me gag. But must have it. Cannot endure those plastic teeth first thing in the morning. Need to come at them from behind sometime later on in the day. So they can't come bouncing down shut on my tongue. Would they? They just might. You can't be too sure.

And lunch? Salad maybe. Yes, with lettuce and celery and those cute radish roses that new paring knife does up so well. But no. Stomach will provide a hundred instant replays of those radish roses. All day long. Free of charge. They only taste good the first time around. No radishes.

Hannah snickered into the room.

No need for all this. I won't need to eat tomorrow. No instant radish replays and no pink plastic gums. When he comes, he brings his own food. And when we get to where we're going, meals are included in the package price. But who is he? You know.

The bells of the church at the end of the block tolled three times.

Who rings them at this time of the night? Never thought of that before. Who then? I don't know. Maybe they work on faith. Like remote control without the wires. But religion doesn't work that way, does it? Sure it does. They've got that man with his finger on the switch. Name is God and he sits on a stool in white robes. In front of the switchboard and closing his white eyes and pushing all those colored buttons. We all jump then. When our button gets pushed. Every one's marked with a name. Or maybe just a number now. Waiting for the finger of God to find it. The finger named . . . what? Death, maybe. God's right-hand man.

Hannah grinned into the dark and settled back into the mattress, letting its cotton-coated fingers work their way up to her skin. She folded the blankets back neatly across the middle of her chest, like a paper napkin neat on somebody's lap. She counted the seconds between each breath, evening it out till it was five every time. Hours passed.

He will come. Who? Death. Didn't your mother tell you that everything comes to those who can wait? I can. And he will.

And what to do about the funeral? Well, I want flowers of course. Lots. Every kind the florist can find. And a coffin grey like seagull wings stuck to rainclouds. Strong wings to bear me up. Gained a few pounds over the years. The wings had better be the heavy-duty brand. Guaranteed for life.

And of course there's the music. Never could make up my mind about that. So many details to fuss around about. So this is how a life ends, is it?

The pillowcase under her neck was growing damp, almost sticky. She pulled it out from under her head and turned it over, cool side up. She cautioned herself to relax, determined that she would not let herself become impatient.

Must make a good impression. Don't push too hard.

A short sharp pinching at her scalp reminded her that her hair was still in pincurls, wrapped up in a pink and green scarf.

Must take them out. Must? Yes, he's coming tonight and metal messes up the machine that finds the bombs and the machine guns. Just a routine Security Check, ma'am, they'll tell me. Nothing to concern yourself about. And we've all got to pass the Check before we can get on the plane. The plane? Well how else do you think we're going to get there, silly? And I've got to pass the Security Check or he'll leave me behind. He might be insulted. Just might not come for me again.

And then what would I do?

Must take these pincurls out right now. Well . . . in a minute.

Hannah reached for the lamp on the night table. Her hand brushed just the edge of the shade. She did not flinch at the crash, pleased by the so-loud noise in her so-empty house. She closed her eyes for a minute to wait.

A minute. A minute.

How many minutes?

Again she heard the church bells. She counted eight rings.

Eight? How can that be? Morning.

The sun shone in through a split in the curtains. Hannah yawned. Unravelling the covers from around her legs, she stood up and yawned again.

Poor sleep last night. Those damn bells would wake up the dead and my lamp fell on the floor. Broke. Now who could sleep through all that?

Breakfast was simple: porridge.

I'll fool you, damn dumb plastic teeth.

She prepared the porridge while still in her nightgown, forgetting to put on her housecoat and slippers. Walking to the back door to bring in the milk, her feet made dry sucking sounds on the floor.

The door was unlocked.

My God.

Hannah steadied herself against the door frame.

What if? What if somebody had broken in? What if somebody, something, had just walked right in and helped themselves? To me.

She slammed the door.

Locked.

The oak panels were strong and safe with no knots.

Locked.

She covered the keyhole with the palm of one hand.

Locked.

A SIMPLE STORY

ONE NIGHT IN A SMALL CITY a man and a woman went out
to a restaurant to celebrate. On the way back, they were nearly
run down by a car that went out of control and rammed into
the window of an apartment building. They were lucky. They
could have been killed.

DESCRIBE THE NIGHT:

The snow begins in the early afternoon, big flakes falling like
shredded paper and with purpose, patiently, so that by dusk,
it is drifting lackadaisically up against picket fences and unsus-
pecting parked cars. By the time the newspapers are delivered
after supper, the wind is up and children all over the city are
dawdling over their homework, peering outside every two
minutes, praying that school will be closed tomorrow. Some
men are already out shovelling. Others are generously offering
to help with the dishes instead, feeling smug and practical
because, if this keeps up all night and then the stupid snowplow
comes, what's the point?

It takes this particular man, Richard, three tries to get out
of his driveway in the suburbs, where there is always more
snow anyway, according to a corollary of that law which causes
tornadoes to hit trailer parks. He is one of those who will shovel
in the morning, cursing and wiping his nose on the back of his
gloves.

This evening has required so many complicated advance

arrangements that they are going anyway, come hell or high water. The dangerous driving conditions only add to Richard's pleasure, making him feel calm and committed.

This particular woman, Marilyn, is waiting for him in the lane behind her downtown apartment building, turtling her chin into her expensive fur coat, sucking on the collar. She is thinking of the time when one of her ex-lovers, Jim's, ex-lovers came for the weekend.

DESCRIBE THE EX-LOVER JIM'S EX-LOVER:

Predictably pert, still on the loose, blessed with a name like Amber, Angel, or Anemone, something like that, the ex-lover Jim's ex-lover spread her perfect thighs, boots, sweater, fur coat all over the ugly couch. Marilyn is thinking of what precise pleasure it gave her when the cat jumped up on the coat and sucked its heart out. She is still congratulating herself on the way she said, "Oh, isn't that cute? He thinks it's his mother! He must be part rabbit," and stuck her head in the oven to check on the chicken.

Marilyn is thinking that if Richard shows up now, safe, not dead in a drift, she will never be nasty again. She feels relieved but eternally obligated when he finally arrives.

Once in the car, she asks stupidly, "Can you see?" and tries to peer through the blizzard by tilting her head at an impossible angle and pressing her face closer to the windshield.

When Richard answers, "Sure, I can see. No problem," she settles back into her coat and sighs, giving herself over to the experienced hands of a God who can always make the visibility better on the driver's side.

Richard didn't buy her the fur coat, although that was the sort of gesture she'd expected at first. In the beginning, she had longed fleetingly for chocolates and flowers, arriving once a week, right on schedule, just when she was feeling the most guilty, the most neglected, or the most fed up with him. They both knew that he had to buy her something: the guilt-assuaging quality of gifts is universally accepted. She took to watching movies about married men, movies with words like "confessions," "secrets" and "lies" in their titles. But they never gave her anything to go on. The only thing these various married men had in common was that they were often found alone in shopping malls at odd hours, buying gifts for their wives and their lovers both, often on the same day in the same store.

DESCRIBE THE GIFTS:

When Richard does bring her gifts, which is seldom enough, he brings her books or records which, he once explained, are more intelligent, more dignified, less likely to give credence to the inherent clichés of their situation. Marilyn makes him sign the books and then leaves them lying around for anyone to see. She doesn't read much but likes to dust them and study the authors' faces on the back jackets. She likes to hold them in her lap like kittens. She plays the records only when Richard is there, for fear of the sadness and regrettable phone calls they might elicit if played at three in the morning with a bottle of white wine. If mink has become melodramatic and embarrassing, hysteria is even worse.

So Marilyn bought the fur coat herself, with a small inheritance she received from her mother's sister, Aunt Louise.

DESCRIBE AUNT LOUISE:

The oldest in a family of fourteen, Aunt Louise was the one who never aged, bought a new bicycle at eighty, got up at six in the morning to bake blueberry pies for the kids, refused to go to the Senior Citizens Drop-In Centre because why would she want to sit around and play cards with a bunch of old people? Aunt Louise could simultaneously make every one of her nieces, nephews and grandchildren, Marilyn included, believe that they were her favorite.

All of the women in Marilyn's family expect to be just like Aunt Louise: growing old without illness, complaint or other damning evidence of decline, kneeling down dead one Sunday morning in the strawberry patch, the juice like sweet blood on her hymn book and hands.

Marilyn was completely surprised when the inheritance cheque arrived. It weighed heavily on her, crazily, dead money in a bank vault, growing interest effortlessly in the dark the way potato eyes grow those waxy white roots in the bin beneath the stairs.

At that time, Marilyn had been sleeping with Richard three times a week for about six months and it was hard on her. She knew she wasn't really cut out for this sort of thing. She was always wanting what she couldn't have: she was always wanting to go grocery shopping with him on Saturday afternoon, to make him take out the garbage, to wash his socks, to wake up beside him in the morning and argue about whose turn it was to make the coffee. She was always wanting him to tell her how stupid his wife was this week, how she was always on him about something, how she didn't understand him, how she was mean to him for no reason. She was always wanting him to say that he was going to leave his wife and then she hated him for saying or not saying it. They took turns believing and not believing that he ever really would.

One day when Marilyn wasn't believing anything Richard told her anymore, she went out and bought the coat without even trying it on. She wanted him to think some other man had bought it for her, some other man who really loved her and would quite happily crawl or die for her.

He said she was silly to squander good money that way. She said it wasn't good money, it was dead money.

She wore the coat with a vengeance, modeling herself after a young woman back home, Mrs. Greene, who, when her husband, a dentist, was killed in a car accident, took the insurance money and bought herself a $50,000 Turbo-charged Porsche. She cruised all over the countryside with the sun-roof open and the tape deck blaring rock and roll. The townspeople were collectively horrified, everyone keeping an eye on her now, asking each other knowingly, "Did you see Mrs. Greene today?" What did they expect her to buy: a hearse? Besides, it could have been worse: the Porsche could have been red instead of black. The more charitable among them suspected she was on the verge of a nervous breakdown, the rest thought she was glad he'd died.

All of these things happened in the small northern town where Marilyn was born and which now seems remote and symbolic, lush with significant memories, gothic.

DESCRIBE THE MEMORIES:

Street corners, weather, storefronts, furniture, meals: any of these are likely to come to Marilyn abruptly, whole and acute, when she is busy doing something else, not watching where she is going.

Waiting for the bus to work one night in front of Mac's Milk, she thinks about an old house on the corner of Cuthbert and Elm Streets, close to her parents' house. She was just a teenager, running home late from a disastrous date with a boy named Desmond who would later marry a girl she knew slightly, Celeste, and who would still later be stabbed to death in a bar fight while Celeste, pregnant with their second child, looked on. The night she thinks about was in February and snowbanks were piled up against the old house. Warm squares of window-light were yellow in the middle of the night. Marilyn stood in front of the old house, lifting and putting down her cold feet like paws, wanting to go in and pour tea from the smoky blue pot she imagined on the table, wanting to pet the cat she imagined on the chair, a grey cat, the kind with fur like a rabbit. Next morning she heard the old man who lived there, Mr. Murdoch, had died in his bed in the night.

Aunt Louise said dreaming of snowbanks was a portent of death. But it wasn't a dream. Those snowbanks around that old house were real as pillows, real and meaningless as these ones piling up all over the city tonight.

DESCRIBE THE CITY:

This is a small, old city which prides itself on its cleanliness, friendliness and well-laid-out street plan, as most small cities do. Richard was born and raised here. His memories are pleasant but do not tell him anything in particular. He doesn't expect them to, being, as they are, a continuum. He couldn't tell you offhand what used to be where the Royal Bank building (twelve stories, tallest in the city, an incendiary issue when the developers first moved in, but once accomplished, it was found to have disturbed nothing much and those who had voted "NO" in the plebiscite did their business there just like everyone else) is now, although, in fact, it was a fish and chip stand where he was always bugging his parents to take him and which still figures occasionally in his dreams.

DESCRIBE THE DREAMS:

In the dream he is a tall teenager dousing his chips with salt and vinegar. His parents are standing behind him. His mother smiles indulgently, his father hands over a five-dollar bill. Behind them, over to the left, two boys he knows from school are fighting on the sidewalk, rolling over and over through cigarette butts, chocolate bar wrappers, ketchup. He steps smoothly

183

around them, pretends he's never seen them before, pretends the one boy, who will die the next spring in a motorcycle accident, has not reached out and grabbed him by the ankle. He shakes the boy's hand off like a puppy and thinks about fish, just walks away.

This is something that really did happen but something which Richard only remembers when he's sleeping.

He also dreams about going to the ballpark. In the station wagon on the way there, he is socking his fist into his new leather glove, breaking it in. Sometimes, after they get to the ballpark and his father parks the car, Richard turns into a grown-up and pitches a no-hitter, while the fans scream and scream, so hot and so loud that they melt.

DESCRIBE THE BALLPARK:

The ballpark is just like any other, with a green wooden fence around the field and chicken wire around the dugouts, where the junior-high kids hide in the winter after school to smoke menthol cigarettes with their mitts on. Richard knows but has never examined the implications of the fact that this ballpark, where he first made love to a sixteen-year-old girl named Eileen who later became his wife, is now the Safeway store where they do their grocery shopping on Saturday afternoons.

Richard is very comfortable in this city and everything about it is just fine with him. When the new shopping malls and suburbs go up, it seems to him that they've always been there. He believes in progress. A small businessman in a small city, he has never been accused of anything, least of all being parochial. Sometimes he feels flawless. Even his affair with Marilyn seems innocent. They're not torturing anyone, not even themselves. They're not like other cheaters. They are in love.

They are driving in the snow past City Hall, a domed limestone building with pillars and colored floodlights, a small fountain into which tourists and townspeople alike toss coins hopefully all summer long. Tonight the floodlights color the falling snow red, blue and green like some curtain poised to go up on a magic show. While they wait at the corner for the light to change, Richard gazes up at the dome with a great deep satisfaction, as if he'd built it with his own two hands.

"Beautiful," he says.

They have passed this building a thousand times and every time he says just that. It is reassuring somehow. Marilyn pats his hand on the gear shift and lovingly agrees with him. Force of habit.

Richard thinks that Marilyn doesn't know that his wife used to work there as a file clerk in the very early years of their marriage, in the happier times.

DESCRIBE THE HAPPIER TIMES:

The kitchen of Richard and Eileen's first apartment was always sun-splashed, the lemon light pouring in through frilly white curtains, running all over the black and white tile floor. There was no dust anywhere. Eileen was at the sink in her apron, the one with the enormous purple grapes embroidered around the hem. Her earrings sparkled and her painted fingernails flitted through the fragrant soapsuds like goldfish. She was always simmering something in a big black pot, spaghetti or chili — they weren't well-off yet, they were still struggling, stirring up gallons of something spicy with hamburger and tomato sauce that would go a long way. They were tired, they'd worked all day. Gliding past each other like skaters on the shiny kitchen floor, they touched unconsciously, sweet pats and slow circular rubs across weary shoulder blades.

Over supper they talked about their friends, their jobs. She was still a file clerk, he was still a cook, frustrated and scheming, dreaming of owning his own restaurant someday. "Poor

Richard," she said. On Friday nights they had a bottle of red wine and made love on the living room floor in front of the TV which flickered like a fireplace. Richard covered himself with her apron when he went to the kitchen to get the cigarettes. Sometimes they talked about having children but Eileen never got pregnant and, as the time for it passed, this was something they stopped discussing and just accepted, going on to other futures, other things.

Marilyn knows about Eileen's job at City Hall (although she doesn't know *how* she knows or why it seems like such a sadistic secret between them) but she doesn't know about the apron.

Marilyn alternates between trying to be more like Eileen (after all, he married her, didn't he?) and trying to be exactly the opposite. The stupid thing is: she has never met the woman, never hopes to, and yet she cannot buy a blouse without worrying that Eileen has one just like it, cannot make Richard a grilled cheese sandwich without worrying that Eileen does it better, just the way he likes it.

Once Richard said, "You sound just like my wife."

They were talking about travelling which Marilyn hates, Eileen too. Richard loves it. What Marilyn said was: "I hate living out of a suitcase and I get constipated in strange bathrooms."

So then she said, "Well, she can't be that bad. You married her, didn't you?" Which, aside from the obvious, also meant: You'll never marry me, will you?

Now she says, "I'm starving."

Richard says, "You're wonderful, you're always hungry, healthy," and Marilyn imagines Eileen existing on clear soup and green salad, pushing the lettuce listlessly around with her fork, looking pale. Eileen is probably one of those people who says, "Oh my, I forgot to eat today." Marilyn can eat a whole medium-sized pizza by herself.

"We're almost there now," Richard assures her.

The city and the streetlights end just past the new Ford dealership. They head north on the highway, singing along with the radio, thinking about how hungry they are, about having some wine when they get there. The restaurant is a new one in the next town where, hopefully, no one will know them.

Because of the storm, there is little traffic on the highway. The headlights of the few cars which do pass them look secretive, urgent or sinister. There is no ordinary reason to be out in this blizzard. Marilyn supposes that they must look suspicious too. Seen through the windshield, the snow appears to be coming and going in all directions at once, even up. It is narcotic and irresistible. She cannot help staring straight into it, as into a fire, until her eyes won't focus and all the flakes are coming right at her, the way the eyes in some pictures, the saddest, most dangerous pictures, are always looking right at you no matter what corner of the room you're hiding in. She wants to go to sleep. Richard, driving steadily, seems fortunately immune to this hypnosis.

Marilyn thinks lazily about driving one night through a snowstorm with her first lover, Luke, to the farmhouse where his best friends, Cheryl and Don, lived.

DESCRIBE THE FARMHOUSE:

Cheryl and Don had rented the farmhouse on Mapleward Road, fifteen miles north of town, for only twenty five dollars a month as long as Don kept the place up. Luke's car was falling apart, back-firing all the way, machine-gunning through the snow. Luke was smoking a joint and turning his head every two seconds to say something to Marilyn. He was one of those people who cannot talk to you without looking at you. Marilyn was frightened, waving him away, pointing at the road which was indistinguishable now from the deep ditches on either side. She was angry too.

"What the hell do you mean dragging me all the way out here in a blizzard?"

It was something to do with money: Luke had some for Don or Don had some for him. Either way it was stupid and probably the result of something illegal they'd cooked up between them.

The farmhouse was set back from the road on top of a hill. The car wouldn't make it up the driveway so they left it down by the mailbox and trudged up the hill towards the old house, which was glowing like a lightbulb in an empty white room.

Suddenly Marilyn wasn't mad anymore. She threw herself down in the snow and made an angel, thinking of what a pretty and innocent gesture it was, something that Luke would remember for the rest of his life. They weren't very happy together anymore and she supposed they were going to break up in a month or two but still: she wanted him to remember her fondly forever.

Don was out in the driveway shovelling. Luke grabbed up the other shovel and pounded Don on the back till the snow sprinkled off him. Don stopped for a few minutes to say hello to Marilyn, stamping his feet and slapping his leather mitts together like a seal. Then they went to work.

Inside, Marilyn and Cheryl played cribbage and listened to Janis Joplin over and over again. She was still alive then, not afraid of anything, they figured, showing few signs yet of letting them all down in the end. "Buried Alive in the Blues." The only heat in the house came from the big black woodstove and they stayed close to it, except when they had to go out back to pee in the snow. Cheryl was wearing a ridiculous outfit that looked beautiful on her: a red cotton dress over a pair of Don's long johns, a purple vest with mirrors on it, rubber boots and a headband. Cheryl made Marilyn feel uptight and out of it in her jeans and new ski sweater.

The men came in and dried their socks and mitts on the stove, drank coffee from metal mugs, made some plans for tomorrow night, nothing special: they'd all go out for a few beers somewhere downtown.

On the way home it was still snowing but Marilyn felt calmer — you were more likely, she figured, to die going someplace else than you were heading home.

A man stood on top of a snowbank waving something at them. They stopped. He had his pant leg in his hand and there was blood dripping from the meaty inside part of his left thigh.

He struggled into the back seat and they drove off. He told them in an English accent over and over again the story of how he'd been just walking along minding his own business when a dog came running out of the trees, chewed off half his leg and kept on running. It was a black dog. It hadn't even knocked him down. He was lucky. It was only one dog. They were said to be running in packs around here. He was just walking along a deserted country road in the middle of the night in the middle of the winter's worst blizzard. Minding his own business.

Marilyn watched him out of the corner of her eye. He was sweating and talking, bleeding all over the upholstery and apologizing. It was probably ketchup. He was probably going to kill them and steal the car. He was probably going to rape her and *then* kill them and steal the car. Luke was driving wildly and trying to think of everything he knew about mad dogs and Englishmen besides that Joe Cocker album. He knew they were supposed to come out in the midday sun. The men laughed at this and Marilyn kept her eyes squeezed shut till she could hear the blood in her ears.

When they dropped the Englishman off at the hospital emergency entrance, he gave Luke a ten-dollar bill and wouldn't hear of them coming in.

Without knowing why it was his fault or what she really meant, Marilyn said to Luke, "One of these days you'll get us both killed."

By the spring, Cheryl was pregnant and she and Don had

taken an apartment in the Franklin Block downtown. After Luke
and Marilyn split up, she and Cheryl became good friends.
Marilyn often went over to the apartment where Cheryl sat in
the Lazy Boy with her swollen feet up, eating Vanilla Wafers
out of the box, watching TV all day in her housecoat. Sometimes
she would get sick and come out of the bathroom wiping her
mouth and groaning. In the kitchen, she cursed and slammed
cupboard doors, craving Corn Flakes. But all the dishes were
stacked in the sink, dirty there for days, because washing them
made her even more nauseated. So Marilyn would do them,
also the vacuuming and the laundry. Cheryl would sit there
eating, licking her lips and her fingers, burping occasionally,
cradling her stomach in her hands.

One day Don came home from work early and Marilyn was
still at the sink, rinsing and wiping and putting away. Cheryl
was asleep with her mouth open. Don came into the kitchen
and took the dishtowel out of Marilyn's hands. He put his arms
around her waist and said, "Thanks. I should have married you
instead."

Now Marilyn is deciding to tell this whole story to Richard
because it just might make him see that there are things about
her he doesn't know yet, things he will never understand, is
not meant to. He likes to say that he knows her better than
anyone else ever will. Sometimes she lets this go by, other
times she says, "Don't be too sure," or, "Oh, you think you're
so smart," which hurts him and he leaves her alone for a while.
But the truth is: he is smart, he is handsome, he is a good lover,
and if he hadn't gone ahead and married somebody else first,
he might have been the man of her dreams.

DESCRIBE THE MAN:

Richard is wearing a brown leather bomber jacket and a
multi-colored scarf which Marilyn knit him last winter to show

there were no hard feelings when he took his wife on a ski trip to Banff. She tried not to think of strangling him with the wool or poking the needles up his nose and, sure enough, the scarf turned out perfectly.

Richard owns a bar and pizza place downtown called Poor Richard's. It is not a sleazy place — it has red and white chequered tablecloths and tacky Italian statues with missing arms and fig leaves, yes, but the cook doesn't wander around with tomato sauce splattered all over his apron and they don't deliver. They have an extensive wine list. They feature live entertainment on weekends which always draws a good crowd.

The waitresses wear tasteful black and red uniforms and do not chew gum, their pencils or their fingernails. Marilyn has been a waitress there for three years. She likes the uniform because it saves her clothes which will then be in good shape for occasions in her "real life" — which hasn't arrived yet, but it will. As a woman, she doesn't think of herself as a waitress *per se*. She never intended to work at the pizza place for this long. She still has a sense of waiting for something better to come along. She does enjoy the job though, working with the public, chatting with the regular customers who tell her their stories a piece or a drink at a time. Take Curtis, for instance. He owns racehorses. You'd think he was a stable boy the way he comes bow-legged into the restaurant in cowboy boots and those tight jeans. Sometimes she thinks she catches a whiff coming off him of sweat and manure, some kind of liniment. He talks to her about odds, purses, jockeys, his lonely ranch. He has been telling her the story for a week now of how his wife walked out on him five years ago.

All Marilyn's customers have something about themselves that they've always been wanting to tell. She listens and gives advice when they ask for it. They say hello to her on the street. She is always a little surprised (but proud) that they recognize her out of uniform and without a tray in her hand.

As a twenty-seven-year-old woman, she doesn't like to think of herself as aimless but sometimes, depressed, she has to admit that that's a good word for it.

DESCRIBE THE WOMAN:

Under her fur coat, Marilyn is wearing a shiny red dress she has been saving for months. It has silver buttons down the front and a black fringe at the yoke. She also has new black boots. Tonight is one of those real life occasions she has been waiting for and she expects to feel satisfied and convinced by the time she gets home. She will not let herself consider the fact that she will be sleeping alone and Richard will be sleeping with his wife. Sometimes when they are together, she cannot enjoy herself at all for worrying towards that moment when he will look at his watch and say, "I have to get home." How does he say it? Afterwards, she can never be sure.

Because of Richard's irregular hours and his being in charge of setting up the work schedule, their rendezvous have never been difficult to arrange. Once in a blue moon, his wife decides to go to Poor Richard's with some of her girlfriends and then Marilyn gets an unexpected evening off. She sits at home in her housecoat, exploring this side of the "other woman" role, crying fitfully if she feels like it, imagining herself getting all dolled up and going down to Poor Richard's and sitting at Eileen's table, introducing herself, buying her a drink, a pizza, a dish of spumoni ice cream, imagining herself pouring a drink over Eileen's head, laughing in her face, telling her that she can have her stupid husband back, he's not that great, she never really wanted him anyway, imagining herself putting her head down on the table or in Eileen's lap (ample, she pictures it, aproned) and going to sleep. But more often lately, Marilyn ends up having a long bubble bath, reading and sipping white wine in the tub, admiring her legs as she shaves them, going to bed early and feeling obscurely pleased with herself. Then, in bed alone, she allows herself the short pleasure of fantasizing about Curtis.

She and Curtis are at the racetrack in the clubhouse which is the exclusive area where the owners and the high rollers sit. He is wearing a white cowboy hat and rings on all his fingers. She is wearing a white dress and sunglasses. They are sipping tall frosted drinks with fruit in them. All of his horses are winning. He wants to buy her a red Porsche.

Or:

She has just impressed Curtis with a sumptuous supper and is piling the dishes in the sink. There is a saxophone on the radio. The steam from the hot water makes her hair curl prettily. Curtis comes up behind her and puts his arms around her waist. He kisses her ear and begins to turn her around slowly, gracefully . . .

The fantasies are abbreviated and unconsummated, to keep the guilt at bay. She is, after all, supposed to be dreaming of Richard and the day he will leave his wife and become forever hers. So she does. All the quirks have been worked out of this fantasy by now, everybody knows their lines and everything fits, including all of his belongings into her little apartment.

Now Richard parks the car a couple of blocks away from the restaurant — a kneejerk kind of subterfuge. Walking away from it, they hold hands and duck their heads down in the wind.

DESCRIBE THE RESTAURANT:

Decorated in the country style, with rustic furniture, old barn wood nailed imaginatively to the walls, quilted gingham placemats and kerosene lamps on the tables, the restaurant is called The Square Dance Room. It is empty tonight, because of the storm, they hope, not the food. Marilyn is still shaking the snow out of her dark hair, thinking that she looks artless and adorable, when the waitress fairly jumps at their table.

Richard says, "You look like a drowned rat," to Marilyn and, "Slow night, eh?" to the waitress, who is wearing a square dance dress the same gingham as the placemats. The skirt sits straight out around her on layers of starched crinoline and bumps into everything: the table, the lamp, Marilyn's arm like a cobweb, as the girl bends to put down the menus and smile sweetly at Richard. Marilyn thinks meanly of a toy clown she once had, the kind with the weighted bottom that bobs and flops drunkenly around at all angles but never falls over on its fat red lips.

They order a litre of house wine and the waitress do-si-does away.

Richard makes a toast. "Here's to our celebration."

DESCRIBE THE CELEBRATION:

Tonight is the second anniversary of their affair. They aren't sure if they should be talking about their past (they've had their ups and downs) or their future together (they don't know what to expect).

When Richard takes his wife out to celebrate their anniversary, they talk about the past year (kind of an annual report) and their hopes for the next year (kind of a prospectus) and then they talk about other things, such as the new lawnmower, the reason the car keeps back-firing, or what color to paint the bathroom now.

At this moment, the food comes. In honor of the occasion, they have both ordered the prime rib, medium rare, with baked potato, sour cream. Marilyn likes it when they order the same meal in restaurants — it makes her feel like they are a real couple, a happy couple with no problems, not a care in the world. It makes her think of those old married couples you see waltzing together at weddings, so smoothly you'd think they were one body with two sets of legs. They dance with their eyes shut, humming.

The food, on plain white crockery plates, is so good they keep smiling at it as they dig in.

Richard says calmly, "I'm putting the house up for sale."

Marilyn thinks calmly, He's leaving her. He's all mine now. I will be stuck with him forever.

Richard says, "We're going to buy a new one, with a swimming pool and a bay window. We're even going to decorate it ourselves this time."

Marilyn can just imagine Eileen squinting at paint chips, caressing upholstery swatches, studying weighty wallpaper books as though they were the Dead Sea Scrolls. She is sucking little mints and making little notes with a thin gold pen. Richard will let her do every little thing she wants and so he will never be able to leave her now. They will live perfectly ever after.

Over coffee and cherry cheesecake for dessert, Marilyn notices for the first time the country and western music playing in the background: "Your Cheatin' Heart," she will recall later, with satisfaction and some inverted sense of justice or triumph. For now, she supposes this is the kind of music that Curtis would like, would tap his cowboy boots to and tease her with when she tells him the story of her romance with Richard. The snow is still piling up outside, sticking to the windows in a festive Christmasy way.

They leave the restaurant and head back to the car. There is a sense between them, swinging somewhere in the vicinity of their clasped hands, hanging there like a purse, of something unsaid but settled. They step through the snow in silence, convincing themselves that it is merely companionable. They are so successful at this that soon Richard is thinking about how they will have just enough time to make love at Marilyn's before he has to go on home and Marilyn is worrying that her new black suede cowboy boots will be ruined for nothing in all this snow.

The car slides sideways towards them out of the snow slowly, so slowly, not like you might think, not like an express train or a charging wild horse. It slides sideways past them, just brushing the tail of Marilyn's fur coat which has billowed out around her at this instant in the wind. It slides into the basement window of an apartment building across the street. The glass shatters all over the sparkling snow and the hood of the car is sucked into the hole. The tail lights are red, the car is green, the snow is white, as Richard and Marilyn are running away.

DESCRIBE THE CAR:

A 1968 Chevy Biscayne Street Racer Special with Posi-traction and a 425 horsepower solid-lifter 427 cubic inch big block under the hood, the car is owned, loved, and now wrecked by a greasy teenager named Ted. He is an unlucky young man and this is just the sort of thing that happens to him. He has just been fired from his job at the gas station and has moved back in with his parents who think that all teenagers are like Ted so it's not really their fault the way he turned out. When he is not cruising in his car, which was a hunk of junk when he bought it for a song, he's working on it. Just when he gets it the way he wants it, he thinks happily of something else that should be done.

Before he hit that ice patch and drove into the window, he was on the way to pick up his girlfriend who works at the Burger King three blocks away.

DESCRIBE THE GIRLFRIEND:

Pinkie is waiting out front of the Burger King, sniffing her long blonde hair to see if the grease smell is gone. She's hoping the snow will wash it away. She has changed into her jeans and has her red uniform in a plastic bag. They are going to see a horror movie. She is thinking about getting a tattoo on her right shoulder, but she can't decide if she wants a butterfly or a unicorn. Either way, her parents will disown her but it wouldn't be the first time.

Ted is ten minutes late. Pinkie hears the sirens but is not old enough yet to be afraid for him. She is just plain mad. She stamps her little foot: if he doesn't show up in five minutes, she will break up with him. She will take a ride with Gerry, who owns a 1966 Dodge Hemi Coronet, candy apple red, and who has been hanging around the Burger King all week, drinking chocolate milkshakes and pestering her to go for a ride. He would take her anywhere, even in this snow. This stupid snow. She can hardly wait till summer.

Ted is thirteen minutes late. Pinkie guesses he got the stupid Chevy stuck in the stupid snow somewhere.

Certainly, she does not suspect that Ted has got the car stuck in an apartment building.

DESCRIBE THE APARTMENT:

In the living room of the cosy apartment, there is a floral hide-a-bed couch and two matching chairs, rust-colored shag carpeting, glass-topped coffee and end tables with doilies, needlepoint pictures of poppies and Jesus on the walls.

Judy, the woman who lives there, is lolling around on the hide-a-bed with her lover, Hal, eating pizza and watching TV. Judy and Hal work at the Bank of Montreal, where she is a teller supervisor and he is the accountant. They have been working and sleeping together for two years. Miraculously, nobody knows this. They have ordered this extra-large deluxe pizza tonight to celebrate Hal's big raise. They feel sinful and smug because they're supposed to be dieting, each trying to lose twenty pounds by Easter. They giggle and relish their various secrets.

Judy and Hal always make love on the hide-a-bed because Judy doesn't feel right doing it in the real bed where she sleeps with her husband, Bruce. She and Bruce sold their house and moved into this apartment after their twin daughters went away to university. They needed the money to put them through, one in medicine and the other in law.

The picture window which Ted's green car comes through is right above the hide-a-bed. Glass and snow are twinkling, sprinkling everywhere and they are all screaming, including the boy in the car, but no one is really hurt. Painless pinpoints of blood well up on Hal's left arm which was in the pizza box when the car hit. One of the broken headlights springs out of its socket and dangles like an eyeball between them. Judy is getting up and tiptoeing through the glass, she is dialling the police, looking for her housecoat, and wondering what on earth she will tell her husband when he finally gets home from work at the bakery which is where he says he is, but Judy has her doubts.

DESCRIBE THE HUSBAND: